The Greek's Bedroom Bargain

The Greek's Bedroom Bargain

A Greek Island Millionaire Romance

Joanne Walsh

TULE

PUBLISHING

The Greek's Bedroom Bargain

Tule Publishing First Printing, March 2019

The Tule Publishing, Inc.

First Publication by Tule Publishing 2019

Cover design by Lee Hyat

ISBN: 978-1-950510-19-1

Chapter One

SHE LEANED IN closer to him. He could feel the warmth of her body against his, her silky, platinum-blonde hair trailing over where the skin of his arm was bared beneath the rolled-up sleeve of his shirt. See the deep, beguiling valley between her generous tanned breasts. "We could go somewhere quieter," she suggested huskily. "Or are you waiting for someone?" Her eyes flicked to the tumbler of Metaxa twelve-star brandy sitting undrunk on the opposite side of the round table. Marco's glass.

"No," Nik replied. "He's not coming." In all likelihood, Marco never would come. But that didn't stop Nik and his adoptive brothers from ordering a drink for their absent younger sibling every time they got together. Gone, but definitely not forgotten.

Nik drained the last of his own brandy and turned to his companion. She'd come over and introduced herself as Elsa, from Sweden, just after Sergei and Dimitri had left, and had wasted no time in letting him know she was available, if he wanted. But he didn't want. Not tonight. Even though Elsa was gorgeous, and he was no stranger to the occasional hookup or brief affair with female tourists vacationing here on the island of Kathos.

He wasn't sure why. Friday night after a heavy week spent commuting between his two bars and nightclub? Maybe. Because he was on call this weekend in Agia Kalamaros as a volunteer captain for the local fire service? Perhaps. Or the growing feeling of discontent with the lifestyle he'd pursued for the last ten years, where pleasure-seeking had filled his downtime, and, every now and then, a vacationing woman his bed? Quite possibly.

When Sergei and Dimitri had been here at *Artemis AK* earlier in the evening to have a couple of drinks with him, they'd ribbed him about Elsa, who'd been sitting alone and throwing him sultry glances, and his uncustomary lack of appetite for what she was clearly offering.

"Hey, *bol'shoy brat*," Sergei had mocked his older brother, using the Russian that had been his first language during his earliest years in a Moscow slum. "What's going on? There's a beautiful girl over there who's mega-hot and ready to trot, and you're just not interested? Are you feeling unwell?"

Nik had rolled his eyes at Sergei's choice of description of Elsa's obvious keenness. "*Mega-hot and ready to trot*? Where did you borrow that from? The lyrics of one of those dance tunes you're so good at churning out for the clubbers of southern Europe?"

"Dance anthems, *brat*, anthems. And I don't churn, I

make music. Music you're quite happy to have played in your club and bars."

Nik had raised his glass in acknowledgement of Sergei's correct observation. He did play the tracks Sergei produced in Athens, which regularly topped the charts with their unique mix of Greek, Russian, and electro-dance influences.

"Could it be you're finally seeing the error of your ways?" Dimitri had asked more seriously. "Realising you'll never meet a woman in a bar or club, or on the beach, who you can settle down with?"

Nik had made an exaggerated show of patting his middle brother's shoulder. Dimitri, who, like him, was Greek by birth, was the most intense of the three of them. "Just like you've never met the woman you want to settle down with *anywhere*, Dimitrios?"

Dimitri had smiled and held up his palms in good-natured defeat. "*Kleidi.* Touché. All three of us know a good woman is hard to find. But there are women out there somewhere, for you, me, and Sergei. You just have to believe."

"Ah. Believing is where you and I part company," Nik had admitted.

Elsa sliding her fingers beneath the front of his partly open shirt jerked his attention back to the present. "So we could go somewhere else and get to know one another...better?" she breathed into his ear, then captured its lobe between her teeth and gently nibbled.

Nik sat still, feeling less than aroused, and more like irritated. He had to stop himself from pushing her away. What the hell *was* wrong with him? Last summer, the combination of her Nordic blondeness and blatant come-on would have had him scooping her up and taking her to his place to have full enjoyment of her spectacular body. But not now. His usual sexual energy had not returned with the new holiday season. But there was still time—this was the first weekend in June. Maybe he just needed to catch up on his sleep, let the temperature rise a little further, and the beaches fill up a little more.

Elsa moving her hand from his chest down to rub at the crotch of his trousers galvanised him into pulling away from her and standing up. She looked up at him, her ice-blue eyes wide with non-comprehension.

"Sorry, *agapimeni mou.* Not tonight." He grabbed his jacket from the back of his chair and moved to leave, briefly stopping to take Marco's glass of Metaxa from the table, raise it in salute to the still-uncomprehending Elsa, and swallow its contents in one gulp. Then he left the building, striding out onto Agia Kalamaros's waterfront, which faced onto the Ionian Sea. A fresh breeze cooled him, bringing with it clarity of thought. He turned to look back at the neon-lit sign of *Artemis AK.* He was proud of his business empire; financially and materially, life was good. He also loved volunteering for the fire station here. But women? As he'd told Dimitri earlier, he wasn't a believer—because he wasn't—in his own ability to commit. The hard, honest truth was, people he'd loved had been taken from him, and that had marked him. Whenever there was a prospect of a lasting relationship, that deep thing within him kicked in, and he made sure to leave before he was left.

He turned back to look out to sea. He stared at the moon rising out over the adjoining island of Lekopolos, casting silvery fingers across the water. Definitely, he was jaded when it came to his love life. Easy sex handed to him on a hot plate no longer excited him. Either he lived as a monk, or he needed more of a challenge…

FRANKIE GENTLY LIFTED the small, skinny cat back into her cage and gave her an affectionate stroke. The feline's ailments—a torn ear, a weeping eye, and sores on her hind legs—had been treated with stitches and antibiotics. Within a week or so, she should have gained enough weight to undergo spaying; though she was only about eighteen months old, the pretty little stray tortoiseshell had clearly had two or three litters of kittens already. But after a bit of TLC, she would be put up for adoption, and hopefully placed with a caring owner.

After leaving the cool, tiled area that housed the cats' cages, Frankie went to wash her hands at the sink in the corner of the adjoining reception room. Staring at her reflection in the small mirror over the basin, she brushed a honey-blonde strand of her straight, shoulder-length hair behind her ear. Six months ago, she wouldn't have believed she would be here at KATS, the Kathos Animal Temporary Shelter, helping Alison Angelis, her mother's old school friend, while she contemplated how to rebuild from the ruins of her life. But back then, though she'd known her marriage was in trouble, she'd had no inkling of what was about to blow up in her face. That Andrew, her husband, would shatter her world a few days before Christmas by telling her he didn't love her anymore, and confessing he was having an affair with twenty-year-old Becky, the junior negotiator at their shared real estate agency. Suddenly, almost everything she'd known had been swept away, and her dreams of starting a family torn down.

She sighed and grabbed her nearby bottle of mineral water, taking a swig. Emotionally, the breakdown of her marriage had been devastating, and she was still a little raw. She'd filed for divorce on the grounds of Andrew's adultery, but there was a way to go before she could look forward to freedom from her husband or to financial stability. Their lawyers in England were wrangling over how the proceeds should be split once their marital home was sold. Frankie also requested that Andrew buy out her share of their business. She sighed again. English divorce law was based on fairness, not equality—with few hard-and-fast rules about who got what—and Andrew was dragging his heels because of it.

But she was trying not to brood too much about it. She was here in Agia Kalamaros to sort her head out, finish healing, and start making plans for her future. Although, she certainly couldn't imagine allowing herself to get involved with a man or having another relationship for a long time to come.

"*Kalo apogevma.* Good afternoon."

The rumble of a deep male voice had her spinning around. She saw the outline of a man standing in the doorway, framed by rays of late afternoon sunshine. "Oh! Good afternoon," she responded.

He entered, and her vision adjusted to take in his sturdy work boots, long, strong-looking legs in navy-blue trousers edged with fluorescent stripes, and a buttoned-up blazer with three stars on its epaulettes that were stretched across broad shoulders—a fireman. *A very handsome fireman.* Her instant attraction to him startled her; she'd thought herself numb to the opposite sex since Andrew had dumped her.

It was a good few seconds before she also realised he was cradling a dog with wild, frightened eyes that was wrapped in what looked like a T-shirt. "Can you deal with this?" he asked crisply in accented but perfect English.

She looked down at the shivering canine in his arms. When the dog let out a whimper, another kind of instinct kicked in. She came forward and allowed the fireman to pass the animal to her. She saw the T-shirt had ruffled up to reveal an angry red wound on its left flank. "What happened?" she asked.

"There was a grass fire up at Skalos, probably started by kids tossing away cigarettes. Some farm outbuildings caught afire. The dog was trapped inside one of them. Can you help her?"

The creature in Frankie's arms was still trembling with pain and fear. She carried her over to the large, metal-topped treatment table in the centre of the room and carefully lowered her down. As she unwrapped the T-shirt, the animal yelped. "It's okay, baby," she soothed, stroking the dog's tan-coloured ear. She looked at the blistered skin again. She wasn't an expert, but she thought it was very likely treatable. "I think so. Her burns look to be first or second-degree partial thickness. I'll ask the vet who does pro-bono work for us to come and check her over, and then we'll look after her until she heals—"

Nothing prepared her for the shock that zapped her when she looked back up. The fireman had removed his uniform jacket and let it fall to the floor; he was standing there naked to the waist. She swallowed to moisten her suddenly parched throat, and couldn't stop herself from devouring the bulging pecs of his upper arms and the ridges of smooth, tanned muscle on his bronzed chest and stomach, which were dusted with dark hair and glistening with charcoal-darkened perspiration…

"Would you pass it to me?"

His low-pitched tones threw her out of her hungry trance. She gulped in some air. "I—I'm sorry?"

"My T-shirt. Could you give it to me, please?"

"Um…yes! Of course." Quickly, she grabbed the garment. Her nostrils were tantalised by its smell of musky male mixed with smoke and a faint undertone of aftershave. She handed it over and wished her eyes weren't gluing themselves back to him as he pulled it over his head and chest, revealing the blazing red, blue, and gold logo of the Hellenic Fire Service, the hard muscles of his abdomen rippling with the effort. Another bolt of sexual electricity shuddered through her. Shaken, not quite comprehending and definitely not welcoming the force of her physical reaction, she stepped away, and, with an effort, returned her attention to the dog on the table and what she should do to make her more comfortable until the vet could come.

"Thank you," the fireman said. "The animal, she was trembling so much. I knew she was in shock, and I had to cover her with something, get her warm."

"You did the right thing," Frankie replied, trying not to look at him anymore. "You said you rescued her from some farm buildings. Does she belong to the farmer?"

"Yes, she was his hunting dog. But he does not want her anymore because she is injured. He was prepared to turn his shotgun on her."

Frankie momentarily froze. "You mean shoot her?" she gasped, straightening up, her eyes meeting his again unintentionally.

He confirmed it with a grimace on his soot-streaked face. "But we stopped him." He extended his large brown hand for her to shake it. "Kontarinis. Captain Nik Kontarinis."

She hesitated, then took it, feeling its hardness and warmth wrapping itself around her fingers, making her totally conscious of him all over again. "Francesca—I mean, Frankie—Worthington. I'm so grateful you intervened and saved her, Captain. Thank you. I guess the farmer wasn't prepared or able to pay for vet's bills."

"I think not." His hand released hers from its firm grip, and she watched as he raised it and rubbed it thoughtfully over his black, buzz-cut hair. He looked around the treatment room. "The money you get to support all this…it comes from tourists?"

"Some of it, yes. We allow them to visit and look around at what we're doing, and we also get donations via our website from all over the world. But we have some local benefactors as well."

He nodded. "That is good to hear. I do not have to tell you this island is overrun with feral cats and dogs. Many Greeks do not believe in neutering their animals."

She could hear a trace of anger in his voice. "It is a problem," she agreed, gently petting the dog on the table to keep her calm. "And, of course, in these times of austerity, when there are families out there relying on food banks to get by, pets are being left uncared for or abandoned. If only we could persuade more people to bring the animals here. We can look after them, find them new homes."

His expression softened as he smiled, revealing even, white teeth. "You and your shelter cannot possibly care for all the cats and dogs roaming around Kathos."

"But we try," she responded, relaxing a little too.

"I have not seen you around here before," he remarked. His eyes narrowed. "I think you must be the daughter of Alison's friend. She told me you were coming to stay."

"Yes, I am." Frankie stopped short of telling him anything more, because she didn't particularly wish to get into *why* she was here with him. Or anyone else, for that matter.

But he was persistent. "How long are you in Agia Kalamaros for?"

"Until the end of the summer."

"And then you will return home to England?"

"Yes." In truth, she had no idea what she would be doing come September.

There was a moment's silence. "I hope you enjoy your time here," he said, which made her hope he'd sensed her reluctance to reveal any more about herself. But then he flustered her again by asking, "What do you do at night? Do you like to go out?"

A frisson of alarm rose in her. Where was this heading? "Well, I…I—" She stumbled over the words. "I'm often on duty looking after the animals in the shelter—"

He scrutinised her like a laser beam. "Do they give you

any time to eat, Frankie?"

She frowned. "Yes, of course…"

"*Kala*. Good. I will take you to dinner then."

His declaration of intent had her defences instantly springing up, and a twinge of fear flared in her chest. No…no! He wasn't asking, he was assuming, and, anyway, she wasn't near ready for this! No way. "Ah…Captain Kontarinis—"

"Nik, please."

"Nik, thank you for asking, but I'm…" She struggled to keep her tone polite and even, because her instinct was to bite out a refusal. "Like I said, I'm nearly always on duty here at the shelter in the evenings."

Sparks danced in his bitter-chocolate eyes. "That is a shame. I know of some very good local tavernas. Do you like fish?"

"Yes, but—"

"Perhaps it is too soon after your arrival. Maybe in a week or two." He hunkered down to retrieve his blazer and rummage in one of its pockets. He stood up, holding a wallet, and then opened it. She watched as he placed a wad of Euros onto the table. "*Parakalo*," he said gruffly, inclining his head towards the dog. "Please use that to cover her treatment. If you need more, let me know. You can find me or leave a message for me at my bar, *Artemis AK*, on the waterfront. I hope she will make a full recovery." His eyes ran over her once more. "And I hope I will see you around."

The dog on the tabletop was struggling to raise up and lick at her wounds. Frankie, her heart thumping nineteen to the dozen, was distracted and didn't reply as she turned back and steadied her. "All right, sweetheart, I know you're feeling very uncomfortable..."

When she looked up again, Nik Kontarinis had gone.

Chapter Two

"YUP, THAT SOUNDS like Nik Kontarinis." Alison resumed chopping the large zucchini, which had been grown by her husband, Pavlos, in the expansive vegetable garden that lay behind their hillside house, shaded by the olive groves Pavlos farmed and adjacent to the converted outhouses of KATS. "Don't get me wrong; he's not some kind of serial seducer, despite what the local gossips say. But when on the prowl, flirtatious, foreign, and female is usually his thing."

"Ooh-kay," Frankie responded thoughtfully as she took in Ali's summary. Since arriving in Kathos, she'd really bonded with her mother's childhood friend, but had learned that Ali, dark-haired, brown-eyed, and in her mid-fifties, wasn't one to pull her punches when giving her opinion about other people. "Foreign and female—I definitely tick those two boxes." She frowned. "But no way was I being flirtatious. Quite the opposite, actually." She took a sip of her wine. "Not that it matters. I refused his invitation. Or rather, his assumption that I would be going out to dinner with him. He seems a bit arrogant."

Ali turned her attention and her knife to an eggplant. "That'll be a first. Nik getting turned down, I mean. He's a millionaire and good-looking, and they just fall at his feet." She sliced some more and then, her head tilted thoughtfully to one side, added, "He is something of a contradiction, though. I've known him for years, and I've always liked him very much. His line of business does mean his life is one long party, and he's used to women throwing themselves at him, but I wouldn't call him arrogant. Just proud, and very driven and determined. And he's also got a heart of gold. As you saw, he volunteers for the fire service. He's a very generous sponsor of the local food bank and the women's shelter in Paragolis as well."

Frankie fingered the stem of her wineglass reflectively. "I saw his generosity when he produced two hundred and fifty Euros for the dog's treatment."

Ali bustled about as she continued with the preparation of a moussaka for that night's supper, nimbly avoiding Nyx, Hades, and Persephone, her three cats, who were sitting nearby on the flag-stoned floor in a patient line, hoping for tidbits to fall their way. "Nik's always been generous. But then, he was adopted and brought up by Ian and Drusilla Brodie Stewart. They were lovely people."

Frankie's ears pricked up. "Adopted? By Ian Brodie Stewart, the thriller writer? I know he used to live on this island."

"That's right. I got friendly with him and Drusilla when

I arrived here. They were very kind about introducing me to the expat community, and also to Pavlos. That was back in his builder days, when he was working on modernising their villa." Ali stopped what she was doing and gazed dreamily out of the kitchen window.

"How old is Nik Kontarinis?" Frankie asked, picking at the bowl of grated cheese that sat before her on the kitchen table, waiting to be added to the sauce for the moussaka.

"Um…" Ali pulled herself out of her romantic recollections. "He must be… Let me see… I arrived here when Nik was about four…so thirty-four, I guess. Ian and Drusilla adopted him when he was a baby. Drusilla couldn't have children, and when Nik was orphaned, they jumped at the chance to take him in. They went on to adopt three more boys. Dimitrios, who was also local and abandoned, I think; Sergei, who came from Russia; and poor little Marco."

That last statement made Frankie stop nibbling at the cheese. "Why poor little Marco?"

"He disappeared at a Christmas fishing festival in Trapazakia when he was just a toddler. It was assumed he was either abducted or wandered off and had an accident." Ali laid down her knife and reached up for the large, copper-bottomed frying pan that hung on a wall-rack. "It will be twenty years this year since he went."

Frankie's eyes widened as she took in Marco's sad story. "Oh, my goodness, that's terrible! Did they never find him?"

Ali shook her head. "Ian was a former crime reporter in

London's Fleet Street. He pulled strings with every police force in Europe, contacted Interpol, and hired private detectives. But no trace of Marco has ever been found. My theory is that he was taken by child traffickers. It happens."

Frankie leaned back in her chair, feeling a little shocked. "Wow. That's quite a past that Nik Kontarinis has: orphaned, adopted, *and* with a missing little brother."

Ali stirred minced lamb, and then the vegetables in the frying pan. "He's a strong man, but there's a lot of baggage there. Buried emotion, methinks. Drusilla, his mother, died a couple of years after Marco went, apparently of a cardiac arrest, but everybody said her heart was actually broken. Nik took her loss very hard. As he did Ian's death from a stroke nine years later."

Frankie watched as the other woman deftly took a wide, oiled earthenware dish and added the cooked lamb and vegetables, then set about swiftly making a white sauce. This Alison poured over the mix in the dish and finished with a layer of the grated cheese, before popping the moussaka into the oven. It smelled delicious, and Frankie's stomach started to rumble. Ali was a fantastic cook.

All the while, her brain was whirring as she thought about Nik Kontarinis's story. It was so dramatic…and tragic. How did you deal with having your baby brother snatched from you, and never discovering what had happened to him?

Without warning, an image of Nik and his naked, glistening six-pack flashed through her mind. She bit her lip hard with frustration, struggling to banish it and the needy ache it aroused low down in her belly. She had to get a grip. It was inappropriate to think that way after what Ali had just told her about little Marco, and, anyway, she shouldn't be interested in Nik Kontarinis or his body, for goodness' sake! Dating, sex, men…she just wouldn't, *couldn't*, be going there right now.

"Penny for them?" Ali wiped her hands, then came over to join Frankie at the table, bringing her own glass of wine. "What's bothering you, hun? You're looking a little pensive. Is it Andrew again? Or maybe Nik Kontarinis?"

Frankie jumped out of her trance and quickly shook her head. "No," she denied, but she could feel the heat of a guilty flush spreading across her cheeks. "I've decided I need to stop feeling bad about Andrew and Becky," she said defiantly, noticing Ali raise her eyebrows knowingly. "I have! It's a waste of my time and energy." she insisted.

"But you've been so cut up about him and her since you arrived here," Ali reminded her.

"I know. But I've got to start getting past it, letting go, haven't I?" Frankie held up her left hand. "Look, wedding and engagement rings removed! I'm no longer Frankie McKnight; I'm Frankie Worthington again. I've resolved I'm going to do my best to be calm from now on whenever I'm in touch with Andrew, and patient while the divorce and financial settlement are being negotiated, even though I'm hating all the legal to-ing and fro-ing. In the meantime, I'll begin thinking seriously about what to do with myself and my future. That's what matters."

"Well, good for you if you can manage it. I do hope Andrew stops arguing and realises he must do the right thing when it comes to buying you out. It's so disappointing that he's getting mean about the financial split, and that the bloody English divorce laws allows him to do it. And, no doubt, he's letting that greedy little tart Becky push him to keep as much back as possible for her benefit."

Frankie couldn't help a grin at Ali's acid assessment; she had related the whole sad story of Andrew's adultery when she'd first arrived. "We'll have to see. To be honest, there's a part of me that would be quite happy to walk away and not bother about the money. But I guess I've got to hang in there, fight my corner, and hope the court will make an equitable ruling."

Ali looked concerned. "Don't give in now. It's about what's due to you—your shares of the house you and he lived in and the business you built between you. Love, you worked so hard for all of that. Just because Andrew couldn't keep it in his pants doesn't mean you should get less than what you're owed. You'll also need some money for whatever you decide to do in the future."

Frankie shrugged. "My lawyer has contacted Andrew's to say we must reach an agreement in the next few weeks and proceed to court."

"Good. I'll keep my fingers crossed for you. And you

know you can stay with us for as long as you want. We love having you." Ali gave Frankie another shrewd look. "But, you know, something is still bothering you, I can tell. Nik Kontarinis, by any chance?"

Frankie puffed out her cheeks and exhaled. She'd discovered she couldn't hide anything from Ali; the older lady was too sharp. "Perhaps...well, yes. When he announced this afternoon that he intended to take me out to dinner, it kind of messed with my head a bit, took me by surprise. I'm just not in the market for dating right now...and definitely not for that kind of commanding alpha-male stuff."

"That's a shame. You'd have a grand time with Nik. He speaks very good English, because of Ian and Drusilla. And I know he'd treat you like a princess if you'd let him take you out. Where's the harm in having him wine and dine you, indulging in some no-strings fun? You've had a rough time recently, and I guarantee he'd cheer you up."

"But you said he's Mr. Flirtatious, Foreign, and Female. I hardly need to be a notch on his bedpost right now. That wouldn't make me cheerful!"

"I don't know he'd treat you like that. After all, you're our guest, and he's a friend of mine and Pav's. And you're not exactly a passing piece of skirt that he's picked up in a bar or on the beach."

"That makes him sound *so* appealing! And hypocritical as well, if he would date me but just shag other women."

"Quite a few of us who know Nik well feel his reputation is undeserved. Sure, he's sown some wild oats, but he just needs to find the right woman."

Frankie rolled her eyes. "Yeah, right, and I'm the Queen of England." She smiled warmly. "You know, it's brilliant being here with you and Pavlos, just what I *do* need. I'm really appreciating your support and the opportunity to chill for a while, make plans. But it's a no from me when it comes to Nik Kontarinis. I'm definitely a single girl for the foreseeable future."

However, later, after dinner, while she was shutting up the animals in the shelter for the night, Ali's words niggled at her and her memory kept straying back to Nik; while she was in the cattery, mind pictures of him stripped to the waist rolled past in an erotic, taunting slideshow. She wished they would cease. She so didn't need it or him right now. He was not for her—too full of himself and only wanting passing flings. She had to focus on getting herself together.

She went into the kennels. Most of the dogs in the caged runs got up from their beds and ran over to her, standing on their hind legs, paws and claws hooking into the netting, tails wagging as they emitted excited barks. She checked that all were okay and had enough water for the night, then stepped back into the doorway, her hand on the doorknob. "Hey, guys, it's time for bye-byes," she called out, then closed the door. She should be heading for bed too. But *not* to dream about Nik Kontarinis. She sighed. How was it that her body was waking up, after months of being alone, and suddenly reacting to the sight of him like he was the hottest thing in the universe? She started walking towards the shelter's exit.

He *was* hot, she allowed. But that didn't mean she was about to scorch herself by jumping from Andrew's frying pan into Nik's fire…

SEATED IN THE cab of the fire truck, Nik hauled the small boy next to him closer and carefully lowered his fireman's helmet onto the child's head. Then he placed his hands on Theo's chubby ones and guided them onto the truck's steering wheel. "We're going to drive the fire engine, *mikro mou*." He turned it a little, pretending to drive. The child chortled with laughter and made siren noises. "Nee-nah, nee-nah!"

Outside the cab, Theo's father looked on, nodding his appreciation. Kostas was the regular captain at the Agia Kalamaros station, a widower single father, bringing up his only son after his young wife had died a year or so ago after losing her battle with breast cancer. Nik had tried to do what he could, paying for Callista to travel to Athens for the best medical treatment, and as an honorary uncle, he always welcomed Theo here at the *klimakia* whenever he was on duty, knowing the four-year-old wanted to be a fireman when he grew up, just like his dad.

"Nee-nah, nee-nah!" As he continued to move the wheel for Theo with one hand, and hold up the helmet that was in danger of sliding down over the child's eyes with his other,

Nik's thoughts wandered back to Frankie Worthington. Since yesterday, he hadn't been able to get her out of his head. He had to see her again. She made him think of a young Grace Kelly, with her cool, sexy beauty—large blue eyes, high cheekbones, pale, clear skin, and smooth, shiny blonde hair. And that sensational slender but curvy body, which had been obvious even under an old T-shirt and jeans.

But she'd refused to go out with him. He smiled to himself. It had been more years than he cared to remember since a woman had turned him down. It was okay, though, a refreshing change—Frankie wasn't easy or only out for a good time. He was happy to work at it; her reserve was the challenge he'd been craving.

His intention had been to check with the shelter later in the week on how the injured dog was doing. Perhaps a visit in person rather than a phone call was in order as a way of meeting Frankie again. Mulling it over, he reached across and blasted the truck's horn, making Theo squeal with delight. Suddenly, the little boy bouncing excitedly beside him delivered a flash of inspiration. Kostas had been talking about getting a pet for Theo, and also a mascot for the fire station—the crew in Paragolis, the island's capital, had recently acquired an Alsatian puppy as theirs. Why not adopt the rescued dog as a companion *and* a mascot? He sounded the horn again for Theo. He'd do anything to make this little boy happy, and if it helped him to win over Frankie Worthington, then all well and good…

Chapter Three

LATE THE FOLLOWING Thursday morning, Nik turned his metallic-bronze Fiat 124 Spider sports into the forecourt in front of KATS. The temperature had leapt up into the eighties, demanding that the soft-top of the car be put down. He was staying at his house in Agia Kalamaros for another long weekend and was in a great mood. He'd be on call at the fire station tomorrow and Saturday night, and was looking forward to some downtime hanging out with his brothers as well. Frankie Worthington had continued to hijack his thoughts and his libido very pleasantly for the past few days too.

He'd decided on a plan of action. Though he wanted her in his bed, he also wanted to get to know her; she was not one of his every-now-and-then vacation encounters. So he'd been thinking of the hidden-away little tavernas he knew where he could take her for intimate lunches and dinners, the quiet, sheltered beaches, or if she wished, the shops, cafes, and clubs in Paragolis, where he had an apartment overlooking the harbour. They could enjoy a long, hot Greek summer together before she went back to England.

He got out of the car, tucked his sunglasses in his shirt's breast pocket, and made his way into the shelter. It felt surprisingly good to be this interested in a woman again—he'd deliberately kept his relationships short and sweet for many years. The prospect had excitement curling in his stomach. But first, he had to overcome Frankie's reluctance to go out with him. Today, his opening gambit would be the injured dog and her adoption by Kostas and the fire station. It was clear Frankie cared a lot about the animals, and he felt certain that when she heard about this, the ice would be broken.

The smell of cleaning fluid hit his nostrils. He halted as he saw the slim figure in front of him. *Kala*. Good. As he'd hoped, she was here, absorbed in washing the terracotta floor of the reception room with a mop, bending forward so that her hair fell in a glossy curtain and the globes of her breasts spilled forwards against the confines of her scoop-necked T-shirt.

"*Chairete.*" She jerked up in surprise, and those pert globes bounced back against her frame. He felt his groin tighten. She wasn't wearing a bra.

She pushed her hair back, surveying him, her forehead scrunching into a frown. "Hello," she responded coolly after a few seconds' pause. "What can I do for you, Captain Kontarinis?"

He ignored the primitive, insistent tugging at his loins. The request, *Call me Nik*, hovered on his lips but didn't leave them. This was one woman who wasn't his for the taking, and he had to go carefully. "I called in to ask about the dog's progress. She is well, I hope?" he responded pleasantly.

"She's doing fine," she said curtly, then returned to mopping the floor.

Ah. Though he hadn't expected Frankie to welcome him with open arms, he hadn't bargained on her being this distant or unfriendly either. Perhaps it was going to be harder than he'd anticipated. He would try discussing the dog's future as soon as he could as a way of breaching her defences. But first, he needed to find out how the animal was getting on. "I am very pleased to hear that. I was wondering if I might see her."

She didn't reply immediately. Instead, she stopped what she was doing, then leaned to shove her mop hard into the drainer of the nearby bucket, making droplets of water spray outwards across the floor. He instinctively winced at the force of the action. She straightened up and rubbed the back of her hand across her brow, allowing him to see the tension that had imprinted itself on her features, turning her previous frown into a scowl. "You want to see her *now*?"

Her response was downright hostile and it immediately rubbed him up the wrong way, all but dispelling his previous good intentions. What was her problem? "Yes, *now*," he countered just as sharply, irritation unusually getting the better of him. "If that's all right with you."

She squared her shoulders. "It's not convenient."

"That is unfortunate. Because I have a proposition for you."

Her eyebrows flew up in surprise, but then she placed her hands on her hips. "As I told you before, Captain Kontarinis, I'm not available for dinner, or any other activity you normally like to indulge in with your lady friends."

Stasou! That was harsh. His jaw clenched as it struck him what she could be implying. "And what activities would those be? Please enlighten me," he drawled, now barely keeping his temper in check.

"I'm not one of your holiday pick-ups," she bit out.

Just as he'd suspected. He gave her a rueful smile. "I see. You've been listening to gossip."

Two slashes of pink flared across her cheeks. "Your reputation precedes you, Captain Kontarinis. We aren't all airhead beach babes out for a two-week romance, you know."

"What would you say if I told you that I want to get to know you because I think you care about more than getting a tan and getting laid?"

Her chin rose. "I would say that's just one of your pick-up lines."

He felt like he'd been slapped in the face. He surveyed her for a few moments, wondering what had happened to make her so damn cynical. He knew that locally there was tittle-tattle about his lifestyle, but why did *she* care so much?

Had some holiday romance gone sour on her in the past?

Suddenly, Frankie Worthington was looking too much like trouble. She was prickly and provocative, and clearly believed those whispers about his so-called reputation. Alarm bells rang. He freely admitted his default when it came to women had long been easy and in control—no emotion, no drama, no complications. Why change now? He could always talk about arrangements for the dog's adoption with Alison later.

"Captain Kontarinis." Her voice sliced through his thoughts. "If it's all the same to you, I would like to get on."

Her tone still held that serrated edge. On the verge of walking away, he stopped himself. When had he ever admitted defeat when he really wanted something? His gaze ran over her as she stood, her hands still planted firmly on her hips. She was stunning. His eyes were drawn back to her breasts as they rose and fell with her accelerated breathing, the nubs of her nipples taut and straining against the thin material of her top. His groin tightened some more. He knew for sure he had to have her. He recalled the first time he'd met her; she'd been modest and unassuming then. There had to be more to her than this shrewish exterior. He just had to keep his cool and persuade her that she'd got him all wrong, by whatever means it took.

And anyway, it would be better if he could push forward and get the arrangements for the dog in place soon. Kostas and Theo were keen to hear news about their prospective new mascot and pet. Taking in a steadying lungful of air, he steeled himself to try again with her.

"Please accept my apologies. It was not my intention to intrude," he began. He gestured down to the floor. "I can see you have much to do here. I should have called ahead and arranged a convenient time. With regard to the dog, I was hoping to see her, and also to talk to you about that proposal I mentioned. I know some people who would like to offer her a home." He went on to explain to her about Kostas, the fire station, and Theo. "It would be great publicity for KATS," he finished. "The *klimakia* would also like to make a generous donation to the shelter for their new mascot, of course."

He saw a flicker of something cross her lovely face, something like hesitation as she considered his proposition. He waited, feeling renewed hope. Now she was looking almost stricken, as if she'd suddenly realised what was at stake, and that her initial reaction to him had been unwise. But, eventually, her poker face slid back into place and she gave the quickest of nods. "All right," she conceded. "Follow me. We'll go and see the dog. But I'd be grateful if you could keep it short and mind my wet floor. I don't want to have to wash it again."

Nai! Even though she was being sharp with him again, she had given way just a little bit. Inside him, a little victory fist punched upwards. He'd have hated to give up too easily. But he didn't show any outward sign of triumph.

She led him—her back ramrod straight, he carefully picking his way across the floor tiles—to a door on the far side of the room. His gaze fixed helplessly on her rear view, her neat backside and long legs encased in skinny jeans—observing how her hips swayed sexily and her buttocks undulated in a heavenly dual motion as she walked. Pictures flooded his mind of making love to her from behind, and he struggled to banish them.

They entered through a low doorway into another long room, walking past rows of roomy cages, from which various feline eyes of many colours watched and the odd plaintive meow came forth. At the end was another heavy wooden door. She stopped to pull it open, and he heard a cacophony of barking start up.

Halfway along the kennel, they halted in front of a run. He peered through the netting. The dog he'd rescued was sitting on her bed, her head on her outstretched paws, a protective collar around her neck, and her big eyes mournful. He hunkered down and spoke softly, "*Ela edo*. Come here, sweetheart." At his call, she raised her head, then leapt up on long, graceful legs and trotted over, poking her nose up against the netting, her tail moving rapidly from side to side. A cursory glance at her flank told him that the wound on her side was healing.

"We put the cone on her to stop her from licking her wound," Frankie explained matter-of-factly in response to his questioning look. "She's been doing well, but she's also been a bit depressed and listless. That's the first time I've seen her actually go to anybody. I think she's pleased to see you. Maybe she recognises you. Do you want to go into the run and give her a pat?"

Nik rose up to his full height. "Yes, I would like to get to know her better."

He noticed Frankie gave him a curious, lingering sideways glance as she unhooked the latch on the run door and gestured for him to step through. What was she thinking? She came behind and shut the gate, then stood at a distance. The dog immediately went to Nik and pushed her wet nose into his proffered hand. He rubbed her tan-coloured head and stroked her silky ears. She was a beautiful creature. "So do we have an agreement about the adoption?"

"Yes, I think so," Frankie replied cautiously. "Though, of course, Alison will need to have final approval." She paused thoughtfully. "Will Kostas and his son mind that she could well have a bald patch on her side where she was burnt? The vet said her fur might never grow back in that area."

He shook his head. "I do not think they will mind at all. And the men at the firehouse will be proud of her because she is a survivor of the very thing they fight."

This elicited the smallest and briefest of smiles from her. But it was soon gone.

"So what is the procedure now?"

"As I said, you will have to get Alison's agreement. We wait until the vet gives the dog a discharge. We will also need to have her spayed; that is our policy. We make an inspection of the home the animal is to go to and then, if all is well, have the prospective new owners visit the shelter a few times to get to know their new pet before we finally release them."

"That all sounds good, very professional. I think you are used to handling prospective clients. What is your job when you are in England?"

Her eyes narrowed warily at his question. "I was an estate agent," she admitted.

"Was?" he couldn't stop himself from probing.

"Yes." She wasn't any more forthcoming. If he wasn't mistaken, something was really bothering her about her life in England. Could that be the clue as to why she was here in Agia Kalamaros, why she was so hostile and withdrawn? He noticed that strained expression had returned and her mouth had become pinched-looking. Instantly, he longed to kiss it, explore it, to coax her lips back to their normal pink lushness, have her willing in his arms…

But she had already started stepping back towards the gate of the dog-run, signalling her desire to leave.

The dog nudged his leg, almost as if she could tell they were about to depart, so he bent down again to give her coat a thorough stroke on her good side. "She is a handsome animal, in spite of her injuries. And apparently quiet and very affectionate, even if she was kept as a hunting dog. I think she will make a fine pet for Theo and a good mascot for the station. Can I leave it with you to talk to Alison and start the process?"

FRANKIE REACHED THE gate and stood by it, her hand raised, her fingers plucking unconsciously at the netting. "Yes, I'll get it sorted," she confirmed. She watched Nik give the dog one more pat. She had to admit he'd been good with her, so gentle, and the dog had immediately gone to him. His proposal for her adoption was really worth considering too; she had a feeling Ali would be delighted. She started to feel a tiny bit of remorse that she'd been so horrible to him when he'd first arrived.

He stood up and came over to join her, standing near and making her feel hyper-aware of him. There was this kind of aura about him; how easy it would be to be drawn to it, like a moth to a flame, to open up and tell him more about herself…get even closer and let him touch her where she wanted him to touch her… His gaze snared hers. "Ready to go?" he prompted.

"*Oh*. Um, yes." She refocused and pulled herself together smartly. "I did say we had to keep it short. I have to get on," she said as crisply as she could.

He followed her back through the kennels towards the reception room. As she walked, she could feel how stiff and high her shoulders were again, to the point where they almost ached. She quickened her pace. She had to get him to leave, or she was going to explode with tension.

"Agh!" In her haste, she slipped and fell heavily onto her behind. One of the flip-flops she'd been wearing had parted company from her foot. Pain and shock raced through her, and she couldn't stop her eyes from filling with tears.

He rushed forward and around her, then got down on his haunches in front of her. She gave an almost imperceptible gasp when he raised his fingers to her cheek and wiped away the moisture beginning to pool there. "Hey, *moro mou*, have you hurt yourself?" he asked gently.

She jerked her head away from his touch. "I'm fine," she lied, and began trying to lever herself up. "I just slipped on a wet patch on the floor."

"I do not think you are." He put restraining hands on her shoulders.

"I said I'm fine. Are you going to get me up?" She hated how bitchy she sounded in her haste to brush away his solicitousness, but she couldn't deal with it.

"Okay." He held his palms up. Then he rose, moved around to reposition himself behind her, and, his hands under her armpits, he supported her until she was upright. For a few seconds, she felt the reassuring steadiness of his body and its warmth as she leaned against him. Once she was standing, he moved away and watched as she took steps to retrieve her wayward flip-flop.

"Ow!" She stopped suddenly, her hand flying around to her lower back. Immediately, he was by her side and supporting her again. She gave in and let him prop her up. He put an arm around her and slowly manoeuvred her around to face him, and then she was looking directly into serious dark brown eyes that were fringed by the most incredible, thick lashes…

"Listen to me, Frankie," he said sternly. "You have hurt and shocked yourself, and you need my help—"

But she wasn't listening anymore. Relaxing into his hold, she moved into a parallel universe where all she could feel were her breasts pressing against his torso, how they yielded to the hard-muscled wall of him, and the musky-citrus scent of him filled her senses. His fingers came up to her chin, then trailed, featherlight, along her jawline. The sensation made her eyes widen and her lips part, and she felt the scorch of suppressed longing flame through her. "It is okay, *pethi mou*," he murmured, his voice as rich as Java coffee, his thumb caressing her jawline and instilling calm. "You are okay. I have got you."

Her tongue darted between her lips, licking them nervously. She was made aware by his intense stare of how that movement transfixed him, and all she wanted in this moment was for him to claim her mouth. Her breath caught expectantly in her lungs as he appeared to battle with himself before lowering his head to kiss her. At first, his lips were gentle on hers, grazing and tasting. Then, when she offered him no resistance, he brought her closer, one of his hands moving to lace into her hair, the other supporting the small of her back.

She gave a needy little whimper and opened her mouth wide, inviting him in, letting him know of her hunger, until their tongues were twined together in passion. A dam of desire burst inside her, and, as he sought her breast, finding it and circling and palming it with increasing pressure, she arched her back, her lower body pressing into his, rubbing against his hardness, knowing the friction would tease and torment him. But he kept his control, reaching for the hem of her T-shirt and sliding under the material to work his way over her smooth belly up to her nipple. When he grasped its stiffness and pleasured it, plucking at it and rolling its length, she responded with a groan. She wanted more, so much more—and it came. Moving to support her buttocks with his other hand, he pulled his mouth away from hers, and, lifting her T-shirt, bared her breast to him. Her own hand went up to its creamy, perfectly rounded paleness and cupped it, offering its raspberry-coloured aureole to him, begging him to taste and suck. He lowered himself to feast upon it, and she sighed deeply when his lips met her skin and drew her in. He lathed her with his tongue, and, once again, she arched and ground herself against him.

On and on, faster and deeper, her passion matched his, until, suddenly, her body wasn't with him anymore. A shock of realisation about what was happening, what she was doing, of where this was going, brutally brought her back to reality. She stepped away, her eyes shining with tears again, her face burning, her breath hitching, her hands clenched. "This is wrong," she grated. "Wrong, wrong, wrong. You need to go. Please leave now!"

Chapter Four

AFTER NIK LEFT, Frankie stood, rubbing at her swollen lips. Whatever had come over her? She heard the sound of a car engine being fired up, and then the screeching of tyres as the vehicle pulled away.

She slumped against the wall, her body still reverberating from his touch. She knew exactly what had come over her. From the minute he'd arrived and she'd seen him standing there, looking beyond gorgeous in tight denims and a pristine white linen shirt, and with a day's growth of dark stubble scuffing his chin, she'd felt that same irresistible magnetic pull as the first time they'd met. It'd scared her, so she'd pushed him away with rudeness. In fact, she'd been downright nasty. Of course, he'd been his usual arrogant self, striding in and expecting to see the dog at the snap of his fingers. But she should have dealt with him firmly but professionally, as her years in real estate had taught her. She should have told him the shelter welcomed visitors Monday through Saturday between two and four in the afternoon, then asked him to come back later—when Alison or one of the shelter's volunteers could handle him.

She felt bad when she thought of how personal she'd been to him, the look on his face when she'd brought up his reputation. It had just slipped out. But she couldn't let him any closer, not with a rep like that. It hadn't helped that she'd also had some devastating news this morning. She'd already been feeling raw, and when Nik had turned up out of visiting hours, stirring up her unwanted attraction to him, it had been the last bloody straw.

She started welling up again. Her lower back ached where she'd landed on it. Could things get any worse? She tried comforting herself that she'd conceded in time that Nik had a right to see the dog because he was paying for her treatment. But when she'd backtracked and taken him to the kennels, it had all gone nuclear. She swallowed, hating her weakness when she'd let him kiss her, touch her like that, and she had responded so...*wantonly*. Now he would think he had her in the palm of his hand, like all his other conquests—the ones she'd been so scornful about.

Her phone, which was lying on a nearby counter, vibrated: Ali texting that lunch was almost ready. When she got back to the house and put her head around the kitchen door, Ali looked up from her food preparations, and, seeing Frankie's tear-streaked face, immediately rushed over to hug her. Frankie let Ali think that it was a combination of the fall and the call she'd had from her mother in England first thing this morning. As soon as she'd heard her mum's anxious voice, she'd known it would be news she wouldn't want to hear.

"Mum, what is it? Is Dad okay?"

"Your father's fine and he sends all his love." Jackie Worthington had hesitated. "Darling, I wanted you to hear this from me. I found out last night that...Andrew is expecting a baby with Becky Protheroe."

"Oh." An arrow of pure grief had pierced Frankie's heart. She was trying so hard to stop caring about Andrew and Becky, but if anything still had the power to hurt her, this was it. She'd struggled to get over her husband's betrayal, and, just when she thought she was almost there, she was knocked back again. To hear he had given another woman a baby—what she had always hoped for—was almost too much to bear.

When she'd told Ali, she'd made one of her acerbic comments. "So Miss Becky's pregnant, is she? Just making sure she's got her claws well and truly into him, and that you could get less money out of him, I suppose."

Frankie had to agree there was more than a grain of truth in what Ali said, but her words had offered no comfort. She'd spent the rest of the morning with it preying on her mind. And then Nik Kontarinis had appeared...

Later, after an afternoon where she'd left Ali and Gladys, an elderly British ex-pat who volunteered at the shelter on a regular basis, to walk the dogs and greet visitors, and she had retreated to the cattery to skulk with the moggies, she got herself into the shower. If only she could scrub it all away.

But the pain in her heart just wouldn't shift, and neither would the flashbacks to how Nik had kissed her, his mouth exploring and ravishing her, leaving her lower belly aflame and her knees like jelly, and wanting him far too much.

The evening meal was a subdued affair. She was totally down in the dumps, though she didn't say anything to Ali and Pavlos about Nik coming to the shelter that morning. The dinner conversation was all about money…or the lack of it—Pav complaining about a big tax bill due any day now, and Ali worrying that one of her major local benefactors, a Mrs Tsitakis, had not come forward with her usual large donation to KATS this year.

Frankie listened, feeling more and more guilty. When the meal was done, she excused herself. "Think I'll go for a walk, clear my head. My back's a little sore and stiff—stretching my legs might help."

Ali gave her a sympathetic nod. "Sounds like a good idea. Why don't you go down to the waterfront, order yourself a nice cocktail in one of the bars, and watch the sunset?"

But Frankie had another mission. Not only had she put the injured dog's adoption at risk, but she'd also let Nik think she was his for the taking. She had to put things—him—right. She knew Ali and Pavlos had worked their socks off to make their olive farm and the shelter pay. But Ali was very honest about how it was always touch and go financially to keep the latter open, and it would be a tremendous coup for them if the fire station were to adopt the dog as its mascot. However, most of all, in a small place like Agia Kalamaros, she would find it hard to avoid Nik. So she couldn't allow him to assume he'd got her where he wanted her—or leave the way open for him to kiss her again while she was this vulnerable and falling prey to the stupid physical attraction that gripped her whenever he was around.

She travelled carefully down the stony incline of the mountainside road to the waterfront. The heat of the day still lingered, and she could hear the hum of cicadas. Her rear still hurt; she'd noticed a livid bruise was forming around her lower back and hip area when she looked in the bathroom mirror. Maybe she should go to the local clinic tomorrow and get it checked out.

When she reached the strip, she looked along it at the brightly lit tavernas and bars. The neon sign of *Artemis AK* stood out. She walked along and stopped outside. Whereas the other venues were mostly constructed from traditional white stone, with blue-painted shutters, *Artemis AK* was an ultra-modern building: cube-shaped, with an open bar on a black slate terrace surrounded by dark wood railings, and dotted with palms and brightly hued tropical plants in square white marble tubs. Coloured mood lighting added to the ambience, and a sound system pounded out dance music. She peered in. Her eyes were drawn into the throng of customers, and she caught sight of a tall, dark figure. Her heart skipped a beat: Nik. It was then that she registered he had a female hanging around his neck. For a moment,

Frankie considered walking away, but instead she took a deep breath, gathered her courage, and mounted the steps; she had to sort this out once and for all.

Holding her head as high as she could, she threaded her way through the heaving crowd to where Nik and the blonde girl stood next to the bar counter. The blonde was very pretty; lithe, tanned, and Nordic-looking, her ample boobs barely covered by a bikini top comprised of small triangles of fabric and leather strings that wound provocatively around her shoulders and torso. Nik's eyebrows rose as he caught sight of Frankie.

"Hi." She raised her voice over the noise of people talking and laughing and the thump of the soundtrack. "Can I have a word?"

FOR A FEW seconds, Nik didn't reply. Then he nodded and disentangled himself from Elsa. The Swedish girl protested and scowled at Frankie, but he ignored her. In fact, he was glad of the chance to cut loose from her; she'd leapt on him as soon as he'd arrived here. Despite her spectacular looks, he'd found she was in reality rather clinging, pouting and dull.

He signalled to the barman, then placed his hand beneath Frankie's elbow and mouthed, "This way." She let herself be guided by him up the wooden spiral staircase. He could see she was climbing it slowly, probably because of that fall she'd had earlier. When they reached the upper level, he opened a door into a private, softly lit room furnished with contemporary, comfortable sofa-style seating, low tables, and large, abstract-art canvases on the wall.

"Please." He gestured to her to enter, then came behind her and around her. He walked over to the giant plate-glass sliding windows and indicated she should join him outside on the balcony.

She did as he bade her and gingerly lowered herself on a chair, then watched while he lit the candles on the table next to her. In their flickering light, he could see she was simply dressed in a pretty short-sleeved blouse printed with a pattern of mauve pineapples and soft, purple-blue pegged trousers that skimmed her ankles over flat, jewelled sandals. Not showy or overtly sexy, but the hint of cleavage, the curve of her hips, and the length of her lightly tanned neck had him aroused all over again.

He could see she was nervous. She rubbed her goose-pimpled arms a few times as if she were cold, when it was in fact a very warm night. She turned away from him to look at the view over the sea and the spectacular red, orange, and purple sunset that illuminated its waters. He wondered why she'd come. To apologise for how she'd greeted him this morning and to ensure that the dog's adoption would go ahead? Or to tell him that the deal was off because of their steamy encounter? She appeared far more personable this evening than she had at the shelter earlier, though he doubted she would readily agree to what he really wanted.

Whichever it was, this visit couldn't be better timed or more advantageous for him. Because, since this morning, when she'd responded to him so instinctively and readily, his plan of action had changed. No more treading carefully. This woman had aroused something strong and primal in him—as he knew he had in her—and he was not about to let that pass…

NIK CAME TO stand beside her. He'd changed his clothes since she'd last seen him. A black T-shirt stretched over his muscular upper physique, while tight, low-slung, battered-looking denims hugged his thighs. The five o'clock shadow on his chin was thicker and darker than before, and his hair was spiky and gelled. She swallowed; he looked drop-dead amazing. But she had to ignore her body's traitorous reaction and concentrate on what she'd come here to resolve.

For the first time, she noticed he was holding a pair of sunglasses, which he now placed onto the tabletop. She saw that one of the arms was slightly bent. He followed her gaze and remarked, "Sadly, I forgot they were in my shirt pocket when we kissed this morning."

So he'd brought it up already. But she wasn't going to be distracted. "I'm sure you can afford a new pair," she dismissed.

"I might keep them as a souvenir."

At that moment, a waiter emerged through the open window and delivered two glasses of Metaxa 12-star to the table, then speedily departed. Nik reached for his and clinked it to hers. "*Stin iya mas,*" he offered, then raised and drank it in one gulp.

She took a sip of hers. The brandy was strong, but she welcomed it as it seeped through her veins, warming and relaxing her for the task ahead. She leaned back into her seat and surveyed him. "What does the toast mean?" she asked in an effort to get the conversation started.

He sat down in the chair opposite. "To our health. How are you this evening?"

"Bruised."

"I am sorry to hear that. You did take quite a tumble."

Even in the combination of twilight and guttering candlelight, she could see his eyes were focused intently on her. For an instant, she fancied she saw something like concern in his liquid brown stare. Then her line of sight was drawn down to his sensual mouth, and she was reminded yet again of how it had moved so skilfully over hers. For her own sake, she had to get on with telling him what she'd come here to say before she dissolved into a pool of wanting again.

"I'm sorry," she said.

"What are you sorry for?" he replied, his brow furrowing.

"Today hasn't been a very good day. You caught me at a

bad time this morning. I wanted to apologise for some of the things I said to you. They were uncalled for."

His mouth quirked upwards again. "Only some?"

She couldn't help smiling back.

"That's the second time I have made you smile today. I think that is quite an achievement as I have not seen you do it very much at all."

She grimaced, then took another sip of her brandy. "Okay, I guess that's true," she conceded. "But like I said, it's been a bad day. I'm not normally miserable. It's just that—" She stopped herself because she realised the alcohol was loosening her tongue.

"Just that what?"

"It doesn't matter."

"Tell me what it is that is bothering you."

She shook her head. "It's not relevant here. Look, I just wanted to make sure that what happened this morning isn't going to stop you from arranging the adoption of the dog."

Nik raised his elbows to rest them on the arms of his chair, then steepled his fingers. A silence ensued as he surveyed her coolly. "It might," he said.

A sudden shiver of unease trickled down her spine. "What do you mean?" she responded quickly. "I did mean it when I said I was sorry."

He fixed her with a hard stare. "When I do business, I aim for what I believe is called a win-win situation; I get what I want, and the other party goes away having gained an acceptable outcome too. I'm sure that when you were an estate agent, you did the same thing."

"Well, yes... But what has that got to do with adopting the dog?"

"You want me to arrange the adoption. She needs re-homing, and I imagine if the fire station makes her their mascot, that would be a very good advertisement for KATS. Yes?"

Frankie felt a drop of perspiration trickle down between her breasts; where on earth could this be leading? "That's correct," she confirmed, and took another sip of her drink to steady herself.

"And, as I recall, I pledged to make a donation to the shelter once the adoption is completed, as has the *klimakia*."

"It was extremely generous of you, and—"

He didn't wait for her to finish but swiftly cut in. "So you will benefit substantially if it goes ahead." He leaned forward slightly, reminding Frankie of a huntsman who had sighted his prey. "But I would need something from you to seal the deal." The corners of his mouth rose upwards as his gaze raked over her. "That you accept my invitation to dinner."

Chapter Five

FRANKIE WAS MOMENTARILY at a loss for words. She watched the smile playing around his lips. Just why was he so keen to have dinner with her and so insistent about getting her to comply that he would give her this ridiculous ultimatum? Had that kiss really meant something to him? She dismissed the idea instantly. He was Mr. Flirtatious, Foreign, and Female; he looked, he took, and then moved on. She reminded herself of her mission in coming here. She didn't want him to think she was his on a plate—a dinner plate! Or was it reverse psychology? That she had sent him packing after they'd kissed and his male pride wouldn't accept it? Whatever, she had definitely been right in her instinct to steer clear of him from the start, whatever else her body had urged her to do.

"I thought I'd made myself plain" she responded tightly. "I don't want to go out with you."

"Perhaps you do not understand what I am proposing," he said smoothly, pinning her with his stare. "Let me lay it out clearly for you. No dinner date, no adoption."

She took in a deep gulp of air in an attempt to calm her

rapid heartbeat, anger starting to rise up from deep inside her. "Oh, come on, Nik! You can't make that kind of stipulation. It's…it's blackmail!"

"I do not think so. My understanding is that blackmail involves forcing someone to do something by threatening them. We are merely negotiating a deal, and I have just stated my terms to you. It is entirely up to you whether you accept them."

By now, she was seething. Who did he think he was, sitting here, so ruthlessly laying down the law? She prepared to leap to her feet, intending to leave as soon as possible, but the speed of her ascent was somewhat curtailed as she was very stiff and achy now. She leaned on the tabletop to steady herself. "You are attempting to coerce me and you should be ashamed of yourself!" she bit out. "Are you really that short of dinner companions?"

He leaned back in his seat, seemingly nonchalant, and folded his arms. "Not at all. As you saw for yourself when we met downstairs, I have an active social life." He tilted his head. "*Oraioitatos*, you are overreacting. Having dinner with me will not be such a big thing. Plenty of business associates celebrate an agreement with a meal." His eyes narrowed. "Or perhaps you are worried about where it will lead? Though I am not quite sure why. You seemed to respond so willingly and uninhibitedly when I kissed you this morning."

She turned her head away without answering. He was needling her, taunting her, trying to get to her…and he was succeeding. She chewed agitatedly at the inside of her lip. Dinner with him was out of the question. It would not be the simple affair he was suggesting. She would be putting herself at his mercy, and she couldn't trust herself not to respond; it would be a date with disaster.

"Perhaps you require some time to think about it?"

She inhaled again, striving for calm. What she required was to get out of here. She turned back to face him. "There's nothing to think about. The answer is no. Now, if you don't mind, I have to be going. It's getting late." She straightened up and made to leave, but the movement had her wincing again, and grimacing.

Immediately, he was up and skirting around the table, halting in front of her. "I will drive you home. It is a long, dark, steep climb up to Alison and Pavlos's house, and you are not in a fit state to attempt it on your own."

Her body went rigid. He was too near for comfort, and she needed to make a quick exit. Without him. She shook her head. "You can't drive, you've been drinking. Call me a taxi."

He didn't budge. "I have had one brandy, that is all. Within the legal limit. Come with me."

Still thrumming with emotion, she thought about skirting around him. She was exhausted, her behind was killing her, and now she was standing up, feeling a little dizzy, probably because she wasn't used to drinking alcohol. It also dawned on her that she'd left her phone at the house, so she couldn't call Ali or Pavlos to come and pick her up. Like it or not, she was trapped. Nik was right; there was no way she could make it up that hill by herself without his help.

She gritted her teeth. It grieved her to have to accept a lift from him, especially after the conversation they'd just had. But if she could just get it over with, she would make sure that, from now on, she would do everything in her power to avoid him. "All right," she accepted tersely.

"Okay, lean on me," he ordered. "Relax. We will take it slowly."

She waved a hand to refuse him, because to be in such close proximity with him could be fatal. He inhaled and his expression betrayed his impatience, but he stepped aside.

"Why don't you lead the way?" she suggested.

He nodded, and she followed him as they left the upper storey without talking. He walked briskly down the spiral stairs, then waited at the bottom of them as she carefully picked her way down, offering her a hand when she reached the last polished wooden step, but she ignored him. He walked over to a door, opened it, and silently ushered her out of the back of the building.

They reached the car and he opened the passenger-side door for her with his free hand, but because she was stiff, she had difficulty turning to lower herself into the vehicle.

"Put your arms around my neck," he commanded.

She opened her mouth to protest. "No, I—" But he took her hands in one decisive move and placed them on his shoulders. It brought her face to face with him. His eyes rested on her mouth, making her lips tingle with remembrance, and his hold was steady as he lowered her down, the muscles in his shoulders rippling and flexing beneath her fingertips.

"Are you comfortable, *pethi mou*?"

She nodded mutely. Her fingers slipped away from his shoulders and dropped primly in her lap. Annoyance and shame, not to mention puzzlement that she should still be so reactive to him after all that had passed between them, overwhelmed her. It had to be the alcohol meddling with her self-control.

He walked around to the driver's side of the vehicle, and, in a series of fluid movements, got in, fired the engine, and accelerated out onto the strip. The top of the Spider was down. As they drove their way up the mountainside, Frankie enjoyed the cool breeze that whipped her hair around, relieving the pressure in her temples. She leaned her head back against the headrest, feeling drained. From the corner of her eye, she watched as Nik effortlessly steered around hairpin bends and potholes in the rough-surfaced road, his profile silhouetted in the semi-darkness. He was the epitome of the handsome playboy. *What would have happened if I'd said yes to dinner with him*? She brushed her traitorous thoughts away. Hell would freeze over before she allowed herself to find out.

At that moment, they passed a set of imposing gates with

lighted carriage lamps set above them, flanked by high, white stone walls overhung with vines and bougainvillea. She heard him say over the roar of the car's engine, "That is my house." With difficulty, she sat up and attempted to look but felt her spine protest, so didn't get to see much as they sped past. She hadn't realised he lived so near to Alison and Pavlos.

"Maybe you will come and visit me there sometime," he said.

She shot his profile a withering glance. "That's not funny. You know it's not going to happen."

He smiled but kept his eyes on the road. "We'll see."

His self-assurance and persistence were truly breathtaking. She lifted her chin. She'd rather the devil himself took her before she'd let herself be vulnerable to Nik Kontarinis. There would be no dinner date; she refused be held to ransom. She would help Alison find another new owner for the injured dog, and the shelter would survive without his patronage.

They swept onto the forecourt in front of the Angelis residence and KATS. Ali had left the outside light on over the front door, and it cast out a welcoming circle of illumination. Nik killed the engine, and Frankie immediately struggled to push herself out of her seat, keen to get inside.

"Wait," he said, placing a stilling touch on her arm and then getting out of the car. He came around to the passenger side, opened the door, then offered her a hand. She had to take it.

"Ooh!" She straightened up and her other hand flew to

the small of her back again.

"You must get that examined first thing tomorrow," he said, catching hold of her. "I can drive you to the Emergency department at the hospital in Paragolis for an X-ray."

"No! No, thank you. I'm sure it's just nasty bruising. I need to apply a cold compress."

They stood for a moment bathed in the lamplight, then she attempted to shake off his hold. But he held her fast and gently turned her to him. Once again, she was alerted to their nearness, the rise and fall of his chest, the heat and strength of his body. She could not to allow herself to be hypnotised by him. She jerked slightly as he raised his hand up to her face and stroked away some strands of her hair that had been disturbed during the car ride. Her breath caught in her throat as his fingers feathered lightly across her cheek. Why was it so hard not to give into the urge to let her face nuzzle into their seductive strokes? With the little resolve she had left, she jerked her cheek away from his touch and stepped back.

"Why do you fight me so hard, *agapimeni mou*? Why do you fight this attraction between us?" he asked softly.

"I have my reasons," she responded flatly.

"And you are not going to tell me what they are?"

"All you need to know is that, for whatever reasons, I can't—I won't—be involved with you."

"Because of my reputation?"

"I didn't like what I heard."

"And you say there are other reasons?"

She mentally cursed herself for that slip. She had no intention of telling him about her failed marriage. "I-I just need to spend some time on my own," she said, stumbling over her words. "Look, I have to go. Thank you for driving me home—"

"He must have hurt you very badly—this man who has made you want to spend your time alone."

Her chin jerked up. "How do you know it's because of a man?"

"Because, *pethi mou*, I know what men are capable of. What has happened to make you so afraid and angry?"

His probing questions made her hackles rise once more. "My past is not up for discussion. Neither is my decision not to have dinner with you."

He gave her a wry smile. "You sound very sure about that."

"I am."

He chuckled. "But you have not denied that there is something incredible between us."

She wanted to refute it, but somehow, because she knew it was the truth, the words would not come. Instead, with a great effort, she turned away from him and walked to the house, her head held high. The heavy wooden front door was unlocked, and she twisted the handle and entered, shutting it quietly behind her. When she was quite sure she was safe inside, and the door was firmly bolted against the outside world and Nik, she slumped against it.

Chapter Six

"IT'S OKAY, NOTHING cracked or broken. Like I thought, I've bruised my lower back very badly. They've given me a crutch and a prescription for anti-inflammatories, and I just need to take it easy for the next couple of days." Frankie waved the walking aid at Ali, who had been sat waiting for her in the X-ray department of St. Nektarios.

"Right, no heavy work for you in the shelter over the weekend then." Ali rose up from her seat. "Come on, Francesca, we'd better get you home. You can phone your mum to tell her that everything's okay. Hopefully, Stavros will have the boiler fixed by the time we've returned."

Frankie noticed how tired Alison was looking. First Pavlos's big tax bill, then Mrs Tsitakis's decision not to give money to KATS anymore, and now the shelter's boiler had failed. A series of financial blows had rained down, and things were looking tough. As she hobbled down the hospital corridor with the aid of her crutch, a cloud of guilt descended over her as she realised that the donations from Nik Kontarinis and the fire station would have come in very handy right now.

On the journey back from Paragolis to Agia Kalamaros, in Ali's battered old Land Rover that had the KATS logo on its side, Frankie sat looking out of the window at the verdant landscape of the mountain valley, brooding.

"I had a call from Nik Kontarinis earlier this morning." Ali's voice broke into her ruminations. "Why didn't you tell me he'd offered to get the dog he brought in the other week adopted?"

What? Frankie was startled. "Oh…uh…he came into the shelter yesterday and talked about it. But we didn't finalise anything." Well, that was true enough, wasn't it? But what the hell was he doing, phoning Ali and telling her about the adoption?

"His idea for the dog to become the fire station's mascot is terrific—great PR for us. And he mentioned he told you that both he and the *klimakia* would be making donations, which will be most welcome." Ali slowed the Land Rover to a halt as they came up behind a farmer herding some goats. She turned to Frankie. "It would have been nice to know that. I could have had one less sleepless night."

Frankie heard Ali's gentle sarcasm and rubbed her clammy palms on her jeans, a sensation of panic gripping at her gut. "Sorry. My backside was so painful, I got distracted."

"He also mentioned he'd asked you again if he could take you out to dinner to celebrate the adoption." Ali swung her a sideways glance, then changed gears, ready to move off now that the farmer had rounded up all his wayward, bleating goats and ushered them onto the side of the road. "Would that be why it suddenly slipped your mind?"

Frankie shifted in her seat so that she could look at Ali, as much as her nagging coccyx would allow her. Her head was reeling. He'd performed another pincer movement on her to get his own way. She wanted to scream with frustration. She didn't want reveal to Ali all of what had gone on. But how else could she avoid getting herself hopelessly tangled up any further in this web of Nik's making? She had to say something. "Oh, Ali, I'm so sorry. You know I don't want to get involved with him. But it's not as simple as that. He…he insisted that I have dinner with him. What was I to do? It felt like he was blackmailing me."

"Blackmailing you? More like keen. It's only an invitation to have a meal with him, love."

"But it's not, is it?" Frankie blurted, emotion bubbling up. She couldn't bring herself to tell Ali the whole story, that he had made the adoption conditional on having dinner. Because shrewd Ali might start asking more questions, and then she'd have to explain about that kiss.

"Aren't you overreacting a little? He also said he wanted to take you out to thank you for looking after the dog."

"That's news to me," she mumbled, hating Nik's skilful spinning and knowing she sounded sulky.

Ali let out a long sigh. "I know you're feeling very raw still. All that's happened with Andrew and Becky, and then the baby; it's been awful and horrible. Look, I know you're going to tell me that I don't know how much because I've been married for nearly thirty years..." She raised a hand off the steering wheel to wave away the protest that was just about to spill out of Frankie's lips. "But, love, aren't you making things worse for yourself by turning into a hermit? Ever since you arrived in Agia Kalamaros, you've been hiding in the shelter, with a face as miserable as a wet weekend in winter. Wouldn't it do you good to start getting out again? How about giving it a go with Nik? He's a good man. He just wants to show his gratitude."

"Well, that's me told," Frankie muttered, stung by the other woman's blunt assessment of her recent mood, and despairing that somehow Nik had turned the tables on her yet again. "I'm sorry about the self-pity. But I'm not having dinner with a man who's tried to coerce me."

Ali reached across to pat Frankie's leg affectionately, while still keeping her eyes on the road. "When did you start taking life so seriously? Look...your mum's old friend is not the most tactful person in the world...but I have to tell you that Pav and I have been quite worried about you since you got here, wondering where the lovely, smiling girl has gone who we used to hear about and see in the photos your mother sent us when she wrote. You remind me of a porcupine, quills ready to defend against assumed predators and denying yourself happiness."

"*Porcupine*! Oh, Ali, I appreciate your concern, but I can't see how having dinner with Nik Kontarinis could be a happy experience."

Ali gave her a wise smile. "You know what? To quote Shakespeare, *the lady doth protest too much, methinks.* You sound very like a woman who is trying to convince herself that the opposite is true. You really do fancy him, don't you?"

Frankie didn't reply as she felt her cheeks flame up. She turned away again to look back out of the car window, feeling even more guilty and cornered. Ali had hit the nail on the head. And Nik had pulled another one over her in his determination to get her to do his bidding. How on earth was she going to let Ali know that the money and publicity she was hoping for wouldn't be forthcoming because she refused to have anything more to do with him?

NIK STRETCHED BACK and let the warm, bubbling water in the hot tub in his bathroom ease the tension in his shoulders. He couldn't lounge for too long; Kostas and Theo would be would be here soon. They were going up to KATS to meet the dog for the first time.

He'd been working with Alison at the shelter this last fortnight to organise the animal's adoption, and Kostas's home had now been examined and approved as suitable for the animal, as had the arrangements at the fire station. Frankie remained a thorn in his side, her fierce rejection of him still rankling. He sighed to himself. As Sergei and Dimitri had wasted no time in letting him know when he'd told the tale to them, he'd let his brain migrate to his trousers for a while where she was concerned. But for the time being, reluctantly, he had put thoughts of her to one side. He hadn't seen anything of her since that night at the bar when he'd offered her his deal.

He wasn't going to stand in the way of Theo getting his new pet and Kostas his station mascot. And in talking to Alison, he'd picked up that KATS was struggling for money, needing a new boiler, and the donations and the publicity that had been promised would make all the difference. So his brain had returned to where it belonged, and he'd made those things his immediate priority. As for Frankie, she was infuriating, stubborn, and passionate. Which only made him want her more—he would return his attention to her soon…

"*Theios* Nik! *Theios* Nik!" He heard Theo's excited voice echo around the hall downstairs. Aspasia, his housekeeper, must have let the little boy and Kostas in. He hauled himself out of the tub and wrapped a towel around his waist, ready to greet them. He went out onto the landing.

"Hey!" He scooped up Theo as the child launched himself at him. "Are you ready to see the dog?"

Theo's expression became serious as he gave a big nod.

"Have you thought of a name for her yet?"

Theo shook his head slowly and solemnly.

"Okay. I am sure when you meet her, you will know

what you want to call her." He looked to Kostas over Theo's head. "Just give me ten minutes to get dressed, and then I will drive us up to the shelter."

As they turned onto the forecourt of KATS in Nik's other car, a four-wheel drive, he experienced a rush of anticipation as he wondered if he would see Frankie. He realised that, despite trying not to, he was hoping he would, and also feeling a little edgy at the prospect. He checked himself. They'd arranged this appointment with Alison. Most likely, Frankie would be nowhere to be seen. Even if she was, she wouldn't want much to do with him.

He wrapped Theo's small fingers in his and led him to the shelter's entrance, Kostas walking behind them. He peered into the reception room.

"Ah, *kalo apogevma*." Alison came forward to greet them.

Nik shook her proffered hand but couldn't prevent himself from glancing over her shoulder, just in case Frankie might be around too. But all he saw was a plump elderly lady with permed grey hair, dressed in a neat blouse and slacks. More disappointment washed over him than he cared to acknowledge.

"This is Gladys," Ali said. "One of our volunteers."

He politely shook Gladys's hand too, then introduced Kostas and Theo.

"If you want to follow me, we will go and see the dog. She's the picture of health now, much more friendly and lively. She recovered nicely after being spayed last week,"

Alison explained in fluent Greek, gesturing towards the entrance to the kennels.

"*Theios* Nik, what does spayed mean?" Theo piped up as they walked through.

Nik hesitated, not knowing how to reply, and looked at Kostas, who pursed his lips. Luckily, Alison was ready to field the question. "It means that the dog has had a little operation, so that when she's ready, she can come and live with you."

When they entered the kennels, Theo pulled his hand away from Nik's and put both palms over his ears as they were met by a chorus of woofs, gruff barks, and keening.

It was then that Nik espied the tall, blonde-haired figure standing alongside the runs, holding the dog on a lead. She was wearing a fifties-style, cornflower-blue cotton sundress with lace on the edges. Its thin straps revealed her sun-kissed shoulders, and it cinched in over a full skirt to show off her slender waist. His heart squeezed—pure Grace Kelly. But what really struck him was how she was smiling broadly as she fought to restrain the animal, which was lurching forward as though she knew two of the strangers in front of her were her new owners. This was a happy, relaxed Frankie he had never encountered before—and she had him captivated and dying to make love to her all over again.

He stood back and gestured to Kostas to take his son to meet their prospective pet. The dog had flopped onto her backside, her tail sweeping across the floor. Frankie dropped down onto her haunches, showing no sign of that fall she'd had a fortnight ago, and, after gently prising his hands from his ears, put a reassuring arm around Theo. She took the child's hand. Whispering reassurance to him, she guided it carefully to the dog's ear so he could stroke her. The animal inclined her head, then started tonguing Theo's palm. The boy giggled. Forgetting his shyness, he looked up at Frankie and said something in Greek.

She looked around, and Nik realised she was searching for him to interpret, which had something inside of him tightening. "Theo said, 'the dog is licking me!'" he explained.

"Okay. Can you tell Theo she is showing him she trusts him? Would he like her to live with him and his daddy?"

Nik came forward to the group and duly passed on the message.

"*Nai!* Yes!" Theo's face cracked into a huge smile. "*Theios* Nik, can we take her home today?"

Frankie gave Theo a hug when she heard Nik's translation. "She has to stay here for a little while longer, sweetie. But you can come and visit her any afternoon you want to get to know her a little better. And then you can take her to your house in a week or two. Does that sound okay?"

Nik knelt down too, his gaze lingering on Frankie. She caught his glance almost shyly from under her lashes. Then she flicked her attention to Theo, who nodded his head enthusiastically when Nik told him the process.

"Why don't we start getting to know her by taking her

for a walk around the front yard? You can help me hold her lead," Frankie said, straightening up.

Nik watched as she carefully guided the little boy along the run and into the reception room, helping him hold the dog as they walked. She was patient, warm, and tender with the child, great with the animals, and with none of the hostility he'd encountered in her before in evidence. He was heartened; there was more to this woman than the beautiful exterior that met the eye, as he'd suspected.

He rose, turned to Kostas, and gave his friend a pat on the shoulder. "I think your boy has found his friend."

Both men and Alison went through to the forecourt too, where Frankie was now helping Theo walk the dog around. At intervals, she showed the boy how to instruct the animal to sit and then walk on and feed her treats as rewards. "I've been training her for you," she said in English. That surprised Nik; clearly, she'd taken a lot of time and care. He decided to go over and thank her.

As he approached her, she looked up. That familiar poker face, which she reserved only for him, slipped back into place.

"Hello, Frankie. I want to congratulate you. It is obvious that you have put a lot into getting the animal well and trained for Kostas and Theo to take her. Thank you."

He could see she appreciated the compliment by the way her expression lightened ever so slightly. "I want everything to go as well as possible."

He nodded. "I'm sure it will." He turned to Theo, who had his arms wrapped around the dog's neck now. "Have you thought of a name for her?"

Theo shook his head, and Nik relayed this to Frankie.

"We named her Até, after the ancient goddess of mischief. She can be quite naughty when she wants to be," she offered. "She stole another dog's dinner the other night."

Nik laughed. "What do you think about that, *mikro mou*?" he asked Theo in Greek. "Does Até sound like a good name for her?"

"Aah-teh." Theo sounded it out. He stopped to think for a moment. "*Nai.*" And then buried his face in her muzzle.

"Then she is Até." Nik turned to Frankie, who was absorbed by the sweet sight of Theo and the dog together. Without thinking, he touched her on the shoulder to regain her attention, his fingertips making contact with the soft golden skin on her upper shoulder. "Frankie—"

Instantly, the atmosphere changed, and she jumped like he'd given her an electric shock. "Oh!"

His fingers fell away, also feeling like a current had passed through them. He swallowed and took a step back.

"I am sorry. I did not mean to startle you. Can we discuss arrangements for Theo to visit Até? The school holidays are starting, so he won't be at kindergarten from next week."

At first, she didn't reply. He thought he detected uncertainty in her, as though she was wrestling with her response. Then her chin lifted and she folded her arms. "You'll have to discuss that with Alison," she said firmly.

Nik searched her face. Her features were set, but her blue eyes were wide...and if he wasn't mistaken, shiny with moisture. Despite her rebuttal, she was struggling, he could tell, with this barely leashed attraction between them.

"I will do that," he replied politely. "Thank you again for your help." He turned on his heel, signalling to Kostas to come and take care of his son as he walked past him. He reached into the breast pocket of his shirt and withdrew his new sunglasses. It could only be a matter of time until she capitulated and he could take her into his bed for as long as it pleased him...he just had to work out how.

Chapter Seven

FRANKIE WALKED ACROSS the main square, heading for the mini-supermarket that was situated on its far side. It was eight-thirty on Sunday morning, before the sun got really hot and lugging groceries home would become an effort.

Her head was still swimming with her encounter with Nik the afternoon before. She'd thought she'd be able to handle it, given that he'd done a complete three-sixty since she'd rejected his dinner ultimatum and gone ahead with Até's adoption anyway. She'd taken Ali's words to heart and had been trying to be more cheerful again. It'd been tough, and she hadn't quite reached carefree yet, but she was getting better about not dwelling on Andrew, Becky, and their baby, and had thrown herself into working hard to get the dog trained and ready in a short space of time. She'd wanted everything to be right for little Theo. But though Nik might have backed off, the sexual magnetism between them hadn't, and her resolve had crumbled within half an hour of seeing him again. Being near him, being touched by him, had just left her aching and confused. She felt incredibly fed up with herself. Why couldn't she stop wanting him, especially since he was so infuriating and arrogant?

She navigated the carousels of beach paraphernalia displayed outside the mini-market and went inside, spotting its owner, Sally Souli, sitting at the till. Frankie had got to know the young English widow quite well now. She was a sweet, gentle lady, only a couple of years older than Frankie, who had been married to a local businessman. Tragically, Manos had died suddenly a couple of years ago. This morning, Sally looked worried, her pretty freckled face scrunched in a frown.

"Hey, Sally, is everything okay?"

Sally looked startled. "Uh…oh, hi, Frankie." She ran a hand through her shoulder-length auburn curls distractedly. "We've just had a delivery of that local goat cheese Pavlos likes. It's over there in the chiller cabinet."

"Thanks. It's on my shopping list." Frankie stopped by the till. "Are you sure you're okay? You look a little upset."

Sally's shoulders slumped as she gave a big sigh. "I had some bad news last night. There's a new mini-market opening down on the strip in the New Year, one of the big chains. The shop fitters moved in this morning." Her voice became wobbly. "It'll be able to offer lower prices than I can, and all the holidaymakers will go there because it's near to their apartments and hotels."

Frankie couldn't hide her concern because she knew Sally might be right. Her store could be eclipsed by a competitor nearer the resort complexes. "Gosh, I'm so sorry to hear that—"

She stopped when she saw Sally's face crumple. "No, don't be," the woman said, hurriedly trying to recover herself. "The villagers will still want to pop in here because it's closer for them. I'll think about stocking extra lines, having price promotions, and maybe I can find the money to expand the space a little out the back, attract new customers. It'll be fine. I—I was just a bit taken aback, that's all."

Frankie patted her shoulder. "If you're sure you're okay?"

"Yes, I'm good." Sally combed through her curls one more time and smiled. "Now tell me all about Nik Kontarinis. I hear that you and he are an item?"

Frankie groaned loudly. "Oh my God, who told you that? There's no way I would get involved with him. I know I'm female and foreign, but he's definitely not my cup of tea."

Sally looked a little sheepish. "Well, you know this shop is the hub for local gossip. Somebody saw you get into his car outside *Artemis AK* one evening a couple of weeks ago." She mustered a smile. "But you shouldn't listen to what's said when it comes to Nik. They've got him all wrong. He's a good man. He just needs a good woman to settle down with."

Frankie gave an exaggerated mock-sigh. "You sound just like Alison. She says I should have a fling with him while I'm here." She reached out a restraining hand to Sally. "But you won't tell anybody that, will you?"

"Of course not. I know what it's like. People say to me that I ought to do the same," she replied sadly. "It's been over two years since Manos died, and I should be getting out and enjoying myself again. But I'm not sure... The shop is open seven days a week, and I don't have the time or energy."

Frankie squeezed Sally's shoulder. "Sounds as if you're not quite done mourning Manos. It's not as easy letting go as some think. I know that. Just take your time. That moment will come when you know you are through it and wanting to be out in the world again. That's what I'm waiting for."

Sally surveyed her with large green eyes. "Thank you," she said softly. "That makes me feel better."

"You're welcome. Now where is that cheese?"

She soon had a basketful of items to purchase. As she made her way back to the till, she saw a noticeboard hung with various community announcements and adverts. There were a couple of small flyers showing properties for sale. One of them had details in Greek and English: a stunning three-bedroom villa overlooking the sea that, according to the blurb, needed completion. As far as Frankie could tell, the outer structure was done, but there was still some work to be carried out internally, and an outdoor pool to be finished. It had a very reasonable asking price. An idea sprang into her head. She headed over to Sally, who was now busy restocking a shelf.

"Sally, the properties on the noticeboard over there—why is one of them being advertised for sale only half-completed?"

Sally turned around, looking a little brighter than she had a few minutes ago. "Since the collapse of the economy here in 2012, there have been many villas lying empty or partially built," she explained. "Their owners couldn't get the money to finish them. Because the crisis isn't yet over, there is a stagnant market and they can be picked up for a song." She pursed her lips thoughtfully. "Thinking of going into Greek real estate?" she questioned.

Frankie gave her an elusive grin. "Let's just say I might have the beginnings of a plan. I'm not sure. It'll need thinking about."

"Perhaps it is a plan I can help you with?" The deep male voice that came from behind her made her spin around. Nik! Talk of the devil! "I couldn't help overhearing your conversation about the half-finished property."

"I thought we'd established that I don't need your help with anything, thank you. Certainly not on the kind of terms you offer," Frankie replied smartly. She turned to Sally, who stopped her stacking, hurried back to the till, and anxiously began scanning Frankie's goods.

Frankie packed and paid, inwardly sighing her relief when she cast a sideways glance and saw that Nik had moved off to the liquor section. "Thanks," she said cheerily to Sally. "See you soon." She left the store.

She started off up the road to home, feeling shaken all over that Nik had appeared like that. As she walked along, a small stone wedged itself between the sole of her foot and her flip-flop. She plonked her bags down and set about removing the sandal to get rid of it, wobbling on one leg. *Bloody stone! Bloody Nik Kontarinis!* No wonder she couldn't get him out of her head if he was always turning up without warning. Well, not always, but this had been the second time he'd shown up unannounced and intruded.

As she swept the debris off the sole of her foot, a shadow blocked out the glare of the sun. Nik stood beside her, clutching a bottle of alcohol. He placed it down on the ground and proffered a hand. She moved to wave him away but lost her balance, and he grabbed hold of her. "Careful, *pethi mou*!"

She fell against him, slamming against his solid, muscular bulk, the fresh citrus scent of his aftershave enveloping her. She felt a convulsion of awareness roar through her and had to turn her head away to try to quell the sensory overload. *Not again*! "I need to put my flip-flop back on," she muttered.

"Okay." He let go of her and went to perch on a nearby low stone wall while she hopped about on one foot again, knowing she looked very undignified, until she had replaced her footwear.

"You need to get a pair of decent sandals," he commented mildly. "Those things are dangerous."

She gave him a freezing look. "Thank you for your advice." She stooped to pick up her groceries. "I must get this stuff home and into the fridge."

"Allow me." He stood up, grabbed his brandy bottle, and came over, then reached and took one of the carriers from her before she could protest.

Avoiding making eye contact, she turned and started trudging up the hill, glowering about the fact that he so often seemed to bring out the worst in her. He matched her stride to walk beside her.

"Are you thinking of purchasing that property, finishing the construction, and renting it out or selling it?"

The probing accuracy of his question made her stop in her tracks. That was exactly what she'd been thinking. "No, I was just curious," she lied, not wanting to engage with him. It was none of his business.

"It's a good idea," he pressed. "Have you any thoughts on how you would finance it?"

"It really was just an idea." She started trudging up the hill again, hoping she could shake him off her tail.

But he was soon back walking beside her. "But you are thinking about it? I would be very happy to invest in your project," he persisted.

She pulled up again and made eye contact. "Really? And what would your terms be this time? Dinner? My head on a platter?"

His sensuous mouth curved up on one side in a lopsided

smile. "*Kleidi, agapimeni mou.* I fear I have asked for that. No demands. Just an offer to back you if you decide to go ahead." His gaze flicked over her. "You are a strong woman, and you know about property. I believe you would make it work. And I can offer you local contacts as well as the money—a builder, plumber, electrician, a lawyer, and accountant. You would probably want to buy to let for the time being as the *yperaxia* tax of fifteen per cent is levied on sales by the government—"

She raised her free hand to stop him. "Nik! It was just an *idea*, that's all." She looked down at her dusty feet. "And even I did want to do it, I hardly think you and I would be ideal bedfellows, do you?" She looked up. Seeing his raised eyebrows and amused expression, she wanted to kick herself. "It's an English expression for partners in a project," she added defensively.

"I know of the phrase," he replied. "But since you refuse to even dine with me, I do not think we will be getting into bed together."

"I'm glad you understand that." She wiped the perspiration that was starting to form on the back of her neck. "It's getting very hot, and I need to get home. It's not far now, so I can take that bag." She gestured to the carrier in Nik's hand.

"I will walk you to your door."

"I would rather you didn't." She kept her hand held out to take the shopping.

"If you insist." He handed over her goods, his fingers brushing hers, then reached into his back pocket and withdrew his wallet, from where he fished out a business card. "Here are my contact details. When you need to talk, just give me a call." When she didn't take it, he leaned down and pushed it into one of the bags, then straightened and gave her a disarming smile. "I will look forward to hearing from you."

THAT EVENING, FRANKIE sat at the kitchen table with her laptop. Her lawyer in England had emailed her to say that Andrew had now changed his stance and wanted to expedite the divorce as soon as possible; he would put the house they'd bought together up for sale and give her fifty per cent of the proceeds on completion. He would also be able to pay her the half-share of their business she was entitled to as another real estate agent, who had been their competitor locally, was offering to buy her out; the two companies would merge and become one larger chain.

Her heart had leapt when she'd first read the email, but now she put her elbows on the tabletop and her head in her hands as reality sank in. She'd got the equable financial agreement she'd hoped for, and she'd soon be free of Andrew in the marital sense. However, it would take time for the house sale to go through, and also for her to receive the money from the business. It looked like her idea about staying on Kalamaros and building up a business buying half-renovated properties, which she would finish and either rent or sell, would have to be put on the back burner; she'd need all of her settlement to bankroll it.

She wondered what Ali would make of Andrew and his sudden willingness to agree to her divorce payout, as Ali was convinced Becky was pulling his strings. Curiosity getting the better of her, Frankie impulsively clicked on her browser and visited Becky's social media page. Her throat constricted when she was confronted by a picture of the girl with Andrew, his hands placed protectively on her stomach, on the now-visible small bump, and read the posts congratulating them on the pregnancy—some of them from people whom she'd called friends when she and Andrew had been together. She sucked in some air, fighting against the negative emotions churning inside her. Now she knew for sure there was no way she wanted to return to the small town where she had lived and Andrew and their families still were. She needed to start over completely afresh. But she had to have some money to do that, and the sooner the better.

Ali came into the room, having just finished shutting up the shelter for the night, with Nyx, Hades, and Persephone scampering behind her; they knew it was suppertime. She picked up a business card that Frankie hadn't noticed, which was sitting on the dresser.

"I found this in one of the shopping bags," Ali said. "Nik

Kontarinis's card. Can I get excited because you and he might be getting together at last?"

Frankie rolled her eyes. "Calm down, dear, there's nothing happening there."

"So how come you've got his business card?"

"I bumped into him when I went up to Sally's this morning to do the shopping. I didn't want it, but he insisted on stuffing it into one of the bags."

Ali came around to stand behind Frankie and surveyed the screen of her laptop. "Ah, the happy couple. Any news on how the divorce proceedings are going?"

Frankie shifted in her chair and folded her arms. "Yes, and it's good and not-so-good news. He's agreed to put the house up for sale and give me fifty per cent of the proceeds. He's also found someone to buy me out of the agency."

"But that's all good, isn't it?" Ali gave a satisfied smile. "What did I tell you? Obviously, he's panicking now about supporting Becky and their child, and he's realised he needs to get the money sorted out."

"I guess." Frankie sighed. "But it's not so good because it looks like I'm still in for a long haul when it comes to getting my share." She unfolded her arms and shut down Becky's page. "Just when I get an idea about what I want to do with my future, and I need finance."

"Oh? Do tell!" Ali pulled out a chair and plonked herself down beside Frankie, then listened attentively as she outlined her plan. "I think that's a fabulous idea. Pav and I were just discussing the other night that we would love you to stay on Kathos. You can live with us, you know that."

Frankie gave her a grateful smile. "Thanks. But any buying won't happen for a while because I have to wait for my money, which is a shame. For one thing, the slump in the property market won't continue forever as the economy here begins to improve. Ideally, I need to strike while the iron is hot and prices are low."

Ali looked thoughtful. She studied the business card still in her hand. "There is one possibility," she ventured slowly.

Frankie's eyes opened wide as she instantly grasped what the other woman was thinking. "Oh, no. No, no, no! Definitely *no*."

"But isn't it worth asking him? He's very rich and a canny businessman."

"If you must know, that was why he gave me his card. He overheard me talking to Sally about the idea and offered to invest."

"Well, there you go!" Ali banged the tabletop to emphasise her obvious feeling of triumph. "Problem solved." When Frankie didn't respond, but folded her arms again and stared at the table, a deep frown creasing her brow, she let out a big huff. "What is the big objection to him? What are you frightened of?"

"I'm not frightened," Frankie muttered, looking up at Ali and feeling uncomfortable because Nik had asked her the same question, and it had hit a nerve.

Ali gave her a rueful smile. "I think you are, honey. Of getting too close to Nik…"

"Because I don't trust him. Why would I want to go into business with a man who has a reputation for throwing women away like used tissues?

"Nik's no saint when it comes to his love life, but as I've told you before, he's not the Lothario of legend. He's just spent the last ten years playing the field. I think what happened with Natassia, his ex-fiancée, put him off commitment."

"Natassia?" Frankie sat up.

"I think you need to ask him about that. Just as you should try talking to him some more about his offer to back your property plan." Ali got up from her chair. "Love, when it comes to business, Nik's reputation is spotless. As for what he does in his spare time, well, my advice would be to make the most of that and take what's on offer. Come on, Miss Porcupine, you're ready to have some fun again. Sleeping with him could be just the thing to help you move on." Her eyes flicked towards the screen saver on Frankie's laptop. "After all, you can't change what has happened with Andrew and Becky. And there Andrew is, wanting to get everything settled for *his* future. He's definitely not mourning the end of your marriage, is he?"

Chapter Eight

NIK WATCHED AS Theo played with Até in the yard at KATS. It was heartening to see; the boy and the dog had become devoted to one another over the last ten days or so, and Theo had visibly come out of his shell. Até had visited Theo and Kostas at home, as well as at the fire station, and she'd been as good as gold. Frankie had trained her well.

He turned and looked at the doorway to KATS, where Frankie leaned against it, watching Theo and Até. She was looking deliciously sexy in the late afternoon sunshine, dressed in a vest that outlined her breasts and shorts that showed her long, golden-brown legs, her blonde hair lightened by sun-kissed streaks. It'd been a couple of weeks since he'd met her at the mini-market, and she hadn't called him. Frustration throbbed at his temples. What was it that was holding her back? How much longer could this battle of wills go on?

She caught his glance and pushed herself off the doorframe, then walked over to join him. "I think we can release Até into Kostas and Theo's care early next week."

"That is good news. Kostas says Theo asks continually when Até can come home," he replied casually, carefully keeping his inner tension under wraps. "Theo has gained so much confidence since meeting the dog."

She nodded her agreement, but he noticed she was worrying at her bottom lip.

"Um…there was something I wanted to ask you about. Can we talk?"

A buzz of anticipation rushed through his veins. Had she had second thoughts about his proposition? "Of course."

"I've been thinking about your offer to invest in my property project."

The tightness in his head was replaced by a rush of adrenaline, but he schooled his features to remain impassive. "I see. Have you come to any conclusion?"

"I'm thinking about staying in Agia Kalamaros and seeing if I can start a business buying, renovating, and selling. Would you consider giving me an interest-free loan to finance my first purchase?"

A short laugh escaped him as he grasped her psychology; she wanted his short-term financial backing, but minimal involvement with him. It could be better than nothing, but maybe there was more to be gained than that. He thought quickly, removed his sunglasses, and pinned her with a stare. "An interest-free loan? And what would be the benefit to me of that, *pethi mou*? I thought you were a smart businesswoman, and we agreed that all deals should be win-win?"

Puzzlement crossed her features. "You said you were interested in backing me financially. Surely this would be more favourable for you, because I'm intending to pay you back—and as quickly as I can."

"How quickly?"

"I will receive a substantial settlement from my divorce."

Divorce? Suddenly, it all made sense. "So my guess was correct. You are a woman who has been hurt by a man."

"I'm not prepared to discuss that," she bristled. "All you need to know is that I will be in receipt of a large payment in due course, and I will repay you for any money you might loan me."

He shrugged. "Time has passed since I made that offer and my priorities have changed."

"Oh," she said, her face falling.

"My preference now would be to receive a return on any investment I make. So this interest-free loan that you suggest does not sound like something I am interested in anymore. Unless—" He smiled and tucked his shades into his shirt pocket. "I am prepared to make the loan to you if you agree to my terms—"

"Oh, here we go again," she said, sounding weary. "Last time we met, you definitely said your offer came with no demands. But you just can't help it, can you? You just have to have your pound of flesh."

He smiled again, not prepared to accept defeat this time. "I am afraid so." He stepped nearer and raised a hand to stroke her hair. It was silky under his fingertips. "On consideration, I need agreement to my terms as a guarantee for the money I'm putting in…as interest on your loan."

She jerked her head away from his touch. "*Not* in front of Theo," she hissed.

He looked over his shoulder. "Theo is very happy playing with Até." His hand went to underneath her chin, which he gently moved so she'd look directly at him again, his thumb stroking her jaw. "This attraction that threatens to explode between us—you cannot suppress it any more. You need to let it happen."

He felt a tremor run through her. "What are you asking for this time?"

"You," he replied softly and inclined his head, wanting to taste her lips. "Your body. We will have an arrangement whereby we work together and sleep together for as long as it takes to renovate and sell the property."

She took a sharp intake of breath. "You know I won't agree to that."

"You will." He moved both his hands to cup her face and kissed her, sensing her lips part to him. "It's what we both want."

FRANKIE STAYED ROOTED to the spot, punch-drunk after what he had just demanded and her stupid body's betrayal as it'd leapt in response to him. She should feel angry with him for moving the goalposts again, push him away, tell him what he was suggesting was wrong. But somehow, she couldn't rouse the emotions or the strength anymore. Right now, standing here, held fast by his caressing hands, she only wanted him to kiss her more.

"So we have a deal, *agapimeni mou*?"

At last, from somewhere, a glimmer of protest sparked in her. "How do I know you'll stick to it?" she challenged.

His hands dropped to take hers and gather them to his chest. "I will have my lawyer draw up a contract for our arrangement that covers my investment, also our partnership in buying and renovating the property and your eventual repayment of the sum, though without additional monetary charges. As for our…intimate relationship, as I have already explained to you, that will be the repayment I seek. In return…" His eyes roamed over her face. "I give you my word. I promise you we will be exclusive to one another, and, as I told you, once the property has been sold, you will be free to go. If you want to."

She moistened her lips. "That could be months. Can you remain monogamous for that long?"

He looked amused at her scornful retort. "I think I will have no trouble focusing only on you." He gave her another lingering kiss. "We will have time to get to know each other and explore our desires."

She swallowed. "I-I need time to think about it." And

she did—to get her thumping heart under control, to let her head rule and not her body, which was so saturated with need for him right now.

"What is there to think about, *agapi mou*?" He freed one of his hands to trail a finger into the hollow beneath her neck. A little shudder ran through her and she trembled again. "I cannot wait to be with you," he whispered.

"Frankee! *Theois* Nik!" At that moment, Theo came running up and flung his arms around his beloved Uncle Nik's legs, followed by a bounding Até.

"Hey!" Nik spun around and picked the child up. "Frankie says Até can come and live with you next week."

Theo beamed.

Frankie took a deep recovering breath. Plastering a smile on her face, she went to grab Até's collar. Her mind whirred. She knew she ought to have rebutted Nik's outrageous proposal, told him where to go. But the wheeler-dealer in her said her property idea was a good one, and he had agreed to give her the loan…only he would exact his own price *interest*, as he had called it.

Was it a price she was prepared to pay? Even after all these weeks of resisting, no matter how much she struggled, her inexplicable craving for him still had the upper hand; right now, she just couldn't tell him an outright *no*.

"I do not wish to wait for weeks again to get your answer." His voice sliced through the turmoil in her head. "Please call me within forty-eight hours and we will arrange to meet."

Chapter Nine

FRANKIE GOT OUT of the taxi in Trapazakia. She was to meet Nik at his bar. His deadline of two days to give him her decision was imminent.

She walked along the cobbled harbour side. The picturesque fishing village was set at the head of an inlet, and less touristy than Agia Kalamaros; there were just a few tavernas and *Artemis TZ*. Even today—a Saturday—it was relatively quiet. She sat down at an empty table shaded from the midday sun by an umbrella outside the bar and waited, just as Nik had instructed. A waiter came and took her order for a small bottle of sparkling mineral water, with ice and lemon. She needed her wits about her.

She took in the stunning view: the fishing and pleasure boats moored along the harbour wall that was constructed out of rocks and the misty-grey outline of Lekopolos in the distance across the azure-blue sea. Though she'd turned herself inside out over the past day and two nights wondering what she should do, she felt calmer and stronger now. She wanted to stay on Kathos, come what may. In the couple of months she'd been here, she'd felt at home, and she was excited for the first time in ages; the idea of embarking on this new property venture was really starting to ignite for her. Apart from anything else, Ali was right—whatever it took, she had to stop mourning her failed marriage, let it go once and for all, and start living. There was no going back, only forward. Having something to work on would be an ideal way of dwelling less on her heartache and starting over.

She sighed to herself. Until her divorce settlement came through, Nik's offer to invest was her only option. But he expected so much in return… *Nik. Infuriating, arrogant, demanding…* How many times had she thought of those words since he'd blazed a trail into her life? Struggled to understand or deny the tingling in her breasts and the liquid heat that pooled low down in her pelvis every time she saw him? If she did dare to throw her lot in with him, agreed to the 'arrangement' and got involved with him for a few months, let him make love to her the way her body demanded, would that be so wrong? She needed to take back some control. If she made sure she stayed detached, was careful not to let him in—and demanded some terms and conditions of her own—she could avoid getting hurt again.

Avoid getting hurt. She closed her eyes for a few seconds as she reflected sadly it was not the kind of relationship she'd envisaged she'd move onto in time, when her heart had healed. A committed, long-lasting relationship that might result in a much-longed-for child—

"*Kalispera.*" His rich tones had her looking up.

"Hi," she said, her breath taken away by how gorgeous he looked in a dark blue polo shirt and tight denims. Though they were only just into the afternoon, a five o'clock shadow darkened his chin, and his hair had that spiky look that always made her want to brush her palm across it.

At that moment, her water arrived, along with another glass for Nik. He sat down opposite her and laid a wallet file with a document inside it on the table. He took his water and raised it. "Am I toasting our partnership?" he asked, his eyes locking purposefully with hers. "Or am I commiserating with myself?"

She didn't flinch from the directness of his gaze. "Yes," she replied, her newfound determination making her sound purposeful. "We have a partnership." She clinked her water against his, then took it back and sipped.

His mouth quirked up at one corner in that way he had, and she was reminded again of how good those lips had felt on hers, making her tummy do a little flip. Although, she would never let him know how much he affected her; as far as she was concerned, this was going to be a heart-protecting business arrangement.

He ran a finger around the rim of his glass reflectively while keeping his gaze fixed on her. "Though I am not surprised that you have said yes, I am intrigued to know what has changed your mind. I thought you regarded dealing with me as like bargaining with the devil himself?"

"Better the devil you know," she replied, glancing at him

from under her lashes.

"But seriously, what did make you change your mind about me?"

She looked away out over the harbour. "I haven't changed it entirely. There are still aspects to you that do not appeal to me." She turned back to him and saw he was regarding her with a frown. She had to ensure he was getting her message that she wouldn't be a pushover.

"The gossip about me—it is still a problem?"

"Is it really only gossip?"

"Mostly."

"Well, be aware that if I get the merest whiff of any hanky-panky behind my back, the sex between us stops immediately."

His brows knitted further together. "What is this hanky-panky?"

"Goings-on; funny stuff; misbehaviour with other women."

"Ah, I understand. I can assure you that I will not have any reason to commit *hanky-panky*, as you call it, while I am enjoying your body."

His frank words conjured up images that made her skin prickle with need, but she quickly pushed them away and faced him with a level stare. "Just letting you know. I also expect you to use condoms on every occasion."

"Of course, *agapimeni mou*, that goes without saying. And it has to cut both ways. There are to be no other men while you are with me."

She rolled her eyes. "We know that wouldn't happen. I'm only just getting divorced after seven years of marriage."

"You did not cheat on your husband ever?"

"No. I had one boyfriend before I met Andrew, and then I was completely faithful to him. Some of us believe in long-term relationships."

He leaned back in his chair. "Yet you are prepared to sleep with me on a short-term basis now." He paused. "You said there are aspects about me that do not appeal to you. What are other things about me that you do not care for?"

"It certainly hasn't been a case of love at first sight, or even second," she batted back, smarting at his observation.

"Who is talking about love, *pethi mou*? Is that what you were hoping for, a *long-term* relationship? Why you pushed me away?"

A gentle breeze from the sea blew some strands of hair into her eyes, and she flicked them away. "Not me. As I told you, I'm in the midst of a divorce. I have no intention of falling in love with anyone, least of all you, for a long time to come. And ours is not an arrangement that could in any way be described as loving."

"But despite this and your views on relationships, you have agreed to it all the same."

She bit her lip. "It suits me to," she replied as coolly as she could manage, glad at last to be able to fire a shot back. "I view it as a means to an end; I really want to get started on the property project."

He surveyed her for a few seconds, an eyebrow raised, then he smiled broadly and reached for the wallet, drawing out a contract. "Then we are in accord. As promised, here is an agreement, in English, laying out the terms of our financial arrangement. Since we last talked, I have decided to buy the property and waive repayment for it from you. Also, you may take the profit when we sell."

She couldn't help her jaw dropping slightly. "You are saying you would finance the whole thing and not expect me to pay you back, *and* let me take the proceeds of the resale?"

He waved a dismissive hand. "You will need the money to invest in your future projects, get a business going."

She thought quickly. "That's very kind of you, but I can't agree to not repaying you. It may take time, but once I have my divorce settlement, I will refund you the full price of the property you buy."

"There is a provision in our contract that it will be your name on the title deed of the villa; legally, you will be the owner. As for the money, I do not need it." He surveyed her, his eyes glittering. "All I want in return is you."

She didn't respond. Instead, she held out her hand, willing it not to tremble and give away her nervousness. "Can I have the contract to read through before I sign it?"

He passed it over. "As long as you sign it before you leave tonight."

She opened her mouth to object, but his expression silenced the words, and she knew he wasn't giving her any leeway. "Then I must check it now." She settled back and started to read through the document. It was short, straightforward, and stated all of what he pledged. She hesitated, then reached for her bag, fished out a pen, and signed it. There. For better, or for worse, it was done. But, she vowed silently to herself, she would repay him for the property once she was in funds; she would not let him buy her, whatever he might think.

When she looked up, he was regarding her intently. "So I will handle the legal and financial arrangements and help you line up any services you need, and you will supervise the refurbishment and the sale of the property. Agreed?"

"Agreed."

"And you verbally agree that we will not only be business partners..." His gaze bored into her. "But partners in bed too?"

"I think the term is bedmates," she murmured, sensing her defences slipping.

He raised his glass once more. "*Se amás.* To us. And our agreement...and to being bed*mates.*"

She clinked her water to his. "*Se amás.*" *And to buying...but never being bought.*

Chapter Ten

FRANKIE ADDED THE finishing touches to her makeup, spritzed her neck with perfume, then stepped back to survey herself in the full-length mirror. Though her uncertainty about tonight's meeting hovered, it was still nice to be able to doll herself up for a change; she hadn't done enough of it lately.

She turned forty-five degrees to make sure her dress looked all right from the side and back. It was black linen, sleeveless and A-line; quite smart, but the low neckline gave it a bit of sass. She'd teamed it with black high-heeled sandals and pearl studs in her ears. She'd eaten a light dinner this evening so that she didn't bloat. Dare she think she scrubbed up well, as they would say back in England?

She got her answer when she went downstairs, and Pavlos gave a low whistle and Ali clapped her hands, exclaiming, "Wow! You look like a million Euros. You'll knock Nik's socks off."

She smiled her thanks, the compliments making her feel braver. Little did Ali and Pav know why she was really seeing Nik this evening. They thought she was going for further talks with him about the property project over drinks. And hoping there might be a touch of romance. But she was going to his house, at his invitation, to have sex with him for the first time. Her heartrate accelerated. There was nothing romantic about it.

A horn tooting outside the house told her the taxi she'd ordered had arrived to transport her to Nik's. "Okay, there's my lift. I'd better get going."

"Have a lovely time," Ali called after her.

As was the way with the local drivers, they went down the mountainside at breakneck speed, causing her to slide about on the car's backseat and grip its edge to steady herself. She was hurtling into the unknown. An uneasy mixture of tension and excitement gripped her. Now she had actually agreed to do this...what would Nik think of her body? What if she froze when she was in bed with him? She'd been inexperienced when she and Andrew had got together as students at the same university, and then married right after graduating. Their sex life had been disappointing and lacklustre. Andrew had started to blame her, and she had blamed herself—

No, no, stop! She was losing her cool. She sat up straighter to stop herself bouncing around and reminded herself of what she'd decided when she'd agreed to this partnership with Nik. It was a means to an end; there was no place for emotion and she had to stay detached. She'd do it to move on to the next stage—and satisfy the physical craving for him that would not go away.

The cab pulled up outside the lamp-lit gates of Nik's place, and she pulled herself back to the present. She got out and paid her fare, resisting a last urge to tell the taxi driver to take her home again. She smoothed down her dress, and then pressed the intercom set into one of the gate pillars. He answered quickly, and the gates glided open.

The house was large, gracious, and old. Its rendered walls were weathered, but its window frames and shutters freshly painted. She walked up the short gravelled driveway, her stomach turning a somersault. He was standing in the doorway, haloed by an overhead light, looking tall, dark, and oh, so handsome. She stopped in front of him. As his gaze ran over her, that lazy, sensual smile curved his lips. For seconds, they stood in silence, and then his hands went to her waist to pull her to him, his eyes blazing in open appreciation, which made a spiral of pleasure rise inside her. "Am I allowed to kiss you in greeting?" he asked. "On the cheek?" He wiggled his eyebrows, and she had to smile.

"Oh, go on then," she assented, and then offered the right side of her face to him. He brushed his lips across her skin, and though he did it lightly, she felt a charge spark down her spine. "You look fabulous," he said, leaning into her, and she felt his lips make contact again. Another current of sensation ran through her, charging her senses and lighting up her nerve endings. Suddenly, all her intentions and misgivings lost their power, and a full-on electrical storm of desire ignited within her instead. She turned to face him. Snaking her hands up around his neck, she gave him a hot, hungry kiss on the mouth.

HE SAT IN a chair in the living room, and she stood before him, her hands folded in front of her. He settled back in his seat. "Undress for me."

She hesitated, then reached for the zip that ran up the side of her dress and slowly pulled it down. Her hands went up to her shoulders and she slid the garment down her arms, so that it fell from her body and pooled around her ankles. His mouth dried and his crotch stirred as he took in her full breasts barely cupped in black silk and lace and her mound, outlined by matching knickers, above long, tanned legs and spike-heeled black sandals.

He rose up and walked over to her. Taking her hands, he helped her step out of her fallen dress. He placed a kiss on her shoulder, and then trailed his lips along to her throat. She shuddered as he gently sucked the skin on the side of her neck. Her head fell to one side, her lids lowering. He straightened and took a step back, his fingers running lightly over the swell of her breasts, down her taut abdomen to the apex of her thighs, where they found her crevice under her silken panties. He touched and rubbed, watching her eyes fly open and hearing her sharp intake of breath.

"That feels good, does it not, *glyka*?" His hand went from her to the fly of his jeans, and, holding her gaze, he unzipped his trousers, letting his erection springfree. He gestured for her to kneel in front of him. Comprehension spread across her beautiful features, and she sank down. She moistened her lips with the tip of her tongue, and he ached with anticipation. After what seemed like a lifetime, she leaned forward and took him into her mouth.

"*Lisous*!" Her hands cradled him as her tongue and lips sucked and glided, making him swell even more. As the exquisite pressure mounted, he fought to hold back, and then gently pushed her away from him. She looked up at him, questioning. "Not yet," he urged.

SHE STAYED KNEELING and watched while he shed his clothes. Her eyes feasted on him when he revealed his naked form, alighting on his muscles as they stretched and bunched. On his taut buttocks, and then his thick, proud hardness as he came to stand, legs astride, in front of her. "Get up," he commanded, and when she did so, he stepped forward and scooped her up in his arms. She let her head fall against his broad chest as he carried her into the hallway and then mounted the stairs, feeling the prickle of rough hair against her cheek and hearing the rapid, rhythmic beating of his heart. When they reached the upper storey, he took her along a landing to double doors that stood slightly ajar. Using his foot, he nudged them open further, revealing the master bedroom.

He came to a halt, and she raised her head to look at him. "There must be pleasure for both of us," he stated and carried her to the king-sized bed, where he placed her down on cool linen sheets and came to lie beside her. He turned and leaned over, her breath catching when his mouth brushed across hers. Then he drew back to search her face with his eyes and sweep his thumb across her cheek. Her lips parted voluntarily. When he kissed her again, she welcomed his tongue as it invaded and plundered.

His hand sought her breast, cupping and kneading it, and she arched against him, relishing his touch. Her need to feel all of his skin against hers grew and she pushed against him, letting him know she wanted to sit up. He helped her. Keeping her gaze on his face, she undid and removed her bra, letting her lush breasts spill free. She saw his eyes following her, devouring her, and she leaned back again, stretching out languorously, feeling the night breeze that came through the open balcony windows caress her nipples, making them point and pucker. Swiftly, he moved over her once more, eagerly running his fingers over their stiff tips, plucking and tugging them. She whimpered, a hot mass of wanting pooling beneath her belly, and he took her mouth again, ravishing it with his lips and tongue.

"Mmm." She rubbed her breasts against him and

moaned against his mouth. Suddenly, the pace increased and one of his hands grasped hers and pushed them together over her head, pinning her, while the other moved to reach between her thighs, tangling with her damp panties. She lifted her rear so that he could drag away the scrap of silk and lace that lay between him and the sight of her sex. He eased her legs open, exposing her. She heard him whisper something in Greek, and then gasped as his fingers reached to part her further and explore her slickness.

Still holding her hands fast above her head, he found, then stroked and pinched at, her core, toying with her until small spasms of sensation made her jerk. He slid two strong fingers inside her, probing and stretching her and milking her juices.

"Please," she begged. "Please..." As the pressure built inside, she closed her eyes, writhing against his hand.

"What is it you want, *moro mou*? Tell me."

She moaned again, unable to form the words.

"Do you want me inside you?"

"Yes...Yes!"

"Okay." She felt him move away from her momentarily, releasing her hands, and then kneel between her legs. She opened her eyes to see him reaching over to the bedside cabinet and grabbing the small foil packet that sat there. Dry-mouthed and spellbound, she watched while he unwrapped the condom and, slowly and deftly, eased it over his length. Then one of his palms reached beneath her to raise her bottom a little, while his free fingers caressed her intimately again. "You are so very wet for me," he whispered. He moved over her once more and, without warning, thrust into her, making her gasp. He stilled. "Are you okay? Do you want me to stop?"

She raised her hand and touched his face. "No."

He started to push once more, slowly at first, then increasing the force, going deeper, making her pulse until she thought she couldn't bear the intensity. But then came the crashing wave of pleasure that washed over her, and then another, and another, until the rush of her climax claimed her and she melted, fisting her hands. He held her tightly as she trembled and panted her release, her breasts rising and falling rapidly.

He trailed kisses along her jaw and down her neck, and her eyes fluttered open, finding he'd raised himself up on his elbows and was staring down at her, still inside her. "Welcome back," he said.

"What about you?" she asked. "Have you…?"

He smiled and pecked a kiss on her lips. "Not yet."

"Well then, you must." She raised her legs and wrapped them around him, drawing him back and further into her. He groaned. Beginning his ascent, his hands gripped hers, his eyes focused on her face. Passion gripped him, and more tremors rolled through her, until he peaked and spilt his hot seed into her with a long, deep roar of release.

They lay together afterwards, he dozing with his arms

wound around her, she with her head tucked between his neck and shoulder, inhaling the musky, post-lovemaking maleness of him and glowing with contentment, savouring the safety and peace of his embrace. Even if it was a bit of a cliché, she had never realised it could be like this—the giving and receiving of pleasure. The intimacy she'd just shared with this man, who had taken her to ecstasy and back, and then to the still, deep waters of fulfilment, had just changed her world forever.

She thought about sex with Andrew and how he'd criticised her figure, her lack of skill, and her inability to orgasm. She smiled to herself. Now she knew the feelings of inadequacy and shame that had lashed her then could be left in the past. Because of Nik. She shifted slightly so that she could plant small kisses on his neck, taste the saltiness of his skin.

She felt him stir. "Are you awake?" she asked.

"*Nai.*" He hugged her closer to him.

"I didn't know it could be like that," she confessed.

He lifted his head slightly to look at her. "What do you mean, *pethi mou*? Was it not good for you?"

"It was perfect," she replied.

He dropped his head back against the pillow. "Thank heaven for that."

She giggled.

"Did your husband not satisfy you?"

Her grin disappeared. "No," she answered honestly. "But

he rounded on me and told me I was the one who was hopeless in bed, that I didn't turn him on."

"He cannot have been with the woman who I made love to tonight. She is deliciously sexy and beautiful."

His words sent a fresh flutter of pleasure coursing through her. "Flattery will get you nowhere."

"That is a great shame," he returned. He rolled over to face her. "Because I was hoping to make love to you again. But tell me a little more about this husband of yours first. You are divorcing him rather than him you, yes?"

She nodded. "Hopefully, it shouldn't be too long now before the *decree nisi* comes through."

Nik took a lock of her hair and gently wound it around his finger. "Did you leave the marriage because of the bad sex, *pethi mou*?"

She sighed. "No. Andrew started an affair with a junior member of staff at our estate agency."

He curled her hair a little tighter around his finger. "I am sorry to hear that. Do you still love your husband after what he did?"

"I'm loving him less and less as each day passes." Her answer surprised her because she realised with a burst of lightness that this was the truth—her feelings for Andrew were diminishing more and more…and new and unexpected emotions about the amazing man who lay next to her were flooding in.

"What are you smiling to yourself about?" Nik probed

gently.

"Oh…just feeling glad to be breaking free. Here's the deal: let's not talk about my marriage. No more questions."

He stared intently at her for a few moments. "Okay."

She reached to kiss him, and he responded with fierce passion before lowering his mouth to her breasts…

Chapter Eleven

THE MINUTE SHE and Nik pulled up in front of the Villa Lemoni, Frankie knew she wanted him to buy it. Painted a light yellow, the shuttered house was set back from the road, between Agia Kalamaros and Trapazakia, and had the most magnificent view of the resort and the sea below from its balconies; from up here, the sunsets would be spectacular. It needed some money spent on it: inside, the brick walls lacked plaster and paint, and wires hung out of them and the ceiling; the floors were basic concrete and required tiling, and the kitchen and bathroom had no fittings. Outside, the pool and hot tub were dug out and the pipework laid, but it needed finishing, and the surrounding patio and garden would have to be paved and landscaped.

"What do you feel, *pethi mou*?" Nik asked after they had walked around a couple of times.

"I think we should go for it," she replied confidently. "It's such a pretty house in the most idyllic location, and though the inside and garden need work, what's here has been done to a high standard." She turned to him, her blue gaze melding with his brown one. "How about you?"

He nodded, looking around him. "I agree. You will just need to decide how you want the décor to look."

"I'm leaning towards light and modern, wooden floors. With a mixture of traditional Mediterranean and tropical themes outside. And some lemon trees."

"Shall I call the owner and make an offer?" He pulled out his phone.

"Try going in at €15,000 under the asking price and see how he reacts," she suggested.

Nik raised his eyebrows. "You drive a hard bargain, but then I know that already."

While he was talking in rapid Greek, Frankie strolled into the kitchen and started planning the layout and look. He appeared at the door and mouthed, "€10,000?"

She gave him a thumbs-up. He walked back into the living area and she went to the doorway to watch as he negotiated, standing with his back to her. From his broad shoulders to his tight butt and long legs, he was magnificent from behind, a testament to his active, physical lifestyle. She recalled the conversation she'd had with him as they'd driven up here in the Spider.

"Are you based in Agia Kalamaros?" she'd asked, realising she didn't know much about her new business and bed partner and wanting to hear more, now that things between them were far more relaxed and easy-going.

He'd inclined his head towards her, but kept his eyes on the winding mountain road. "I divide my time between here and Paragolis. As you know, I own two bars, *Artemis AK* and *Artemis TZ* in Trapazakia. I have a nightclub in Paragolis, which is called *Iris*. I have a house in Agia Kalamaros and an apartment in Paragolis. I have also been considering setting up a small company letting out and selling holiday villas."

"Wow," Frankie had replied, impressed. "Now I understand why you are willing to invest in me and this property. You've quite the business empire already. And you still manage to fit in being a voluntary firefighter?"

"It is important to me. Kostas is very flexible about my hours."

"So you fight mainly grass fires?"

"There are forest fires too, property fires…car accidents. In a mountainous area like this, there can be floods and landslides, especially in the winter, so we are on hand to help with those."

Despite the breezy ride in the open-topped Spider, a warm flush had washed through her as she'd thought about how hard and muscular his body had felt against hers when they'd made love, and she'd commented, "I suppose you have to keep very fit for all of that?"

"I have a mini gym in my house in Agia Kalamaros, and weights at the Paragolis apartment to keep me topped up."

He ended the call and spun around, bringing her back to earth. "We have a deal, at €10,000 lower than the original asking price. Is that okay with you?"

"Yay!" Delighted, she rushed forward and flung her arms

around his neck. He welcomed her exuberance, catching hold of her and lifting her high, his big hands supporting her bottom. She wrapped her legs around his hips.

"Hey," he said softly, looking up at her, then dropping his grip a little so she slid down and her face became level with his. "So, my little witch, we have our first property to work on together—"

"*Witch*? I know I was a bit horrible when you first met me, but hopefully since then you've been able to see that I'm not so bad."

"I am thinking a witch is a sorceress, and you have enchanted me. What else can a witch be?"

She blushed at his description. "In the UK, a witch can also mean a woman who's a bit of a bitch. Which perhaps I was at the beginning."

He laughed. "I never thought you were a bitch. Infuriating and frustrating maybe, but not a bitch."

She shared his laughter. "That's funny. I thought pretty much the same about you. Oh, and you can add in arrogant."

He leaned in and stole a quick peck on her mouth. "Arrogant, *gylka*? I do not recognise that description," he growled. "But hot and horny as hell because I have a beautiful, sexy witch in my arms I can accept." His mouth claimed hers roughly and she melted into him, matching the force of his kiss.

SHE ALLOWED HIM to help her out of the Spider outside *Artemis AK*. He had phoned both Dimitri and Sergei from the Villa Lemoni and asked his brothers to meet them at the bar to help celebrate its purchase. She'd been really pleased and surprised that he wanted to introduce her to his family.

Once inside, she saw two men who were equally as handsome as Nik sitting at a table in an alcoved area. "*Chairete*!" Both stood in welcome, and she realised they were as tall as he was too.

When they got to the table, one of the men, who was leaner and less thickset than Nik, with short, jet-black hair, large dark eyes, and a strong nose and mouth, took her hand and kissed its back. "It is a pleasure to meet such a beautiful woman," he said. The other man bowed, making his long, dark brown hair fall forward over his face. His deep-set blue eyes had a slight slant to them and his high, sculpted cheekbones gave him a noble air. "My brother told us you were beautiful, but he did not do you justice." He spoke with what sounded like a Russian accent.

Frankie coloured up at this sweep of compliments. "Thank you."

"This is Dimitri Bekatoros." Nik gestured to the dark man. "And Sergei Alkaev." The latter gave another small bow. "My brothers. Dimitri lives in Skalos, and Sergei sometimes lives in Agia Kalamaros when he's not in Athens."

When they were all seated and Nik had signalled for Frankie to be brought the gin and tonic she'd requested, she noticed there was a solitary brandy sitting on the other side of the table in front of another empty chair. "Is someone else joining us?" she asked.

The mood amongst the brothers immediately became sombre. "No," Nik told her heavily. "Whenever Dimitri, Sergei, and I meet, it is our custom to order a drink for our little brother, Marco." He sighed. "He went missing twenty years ago, and, though we keep searching, he's never been found. Perhaps he never will be. But we like to keep his memory and the hope alive."

Frankie gave him a sympathetic nod. "Alison told me what happened. I'm so sorry."

At that moment, her drink arrived. Sergei raised his glass. "To our *brat*, Marco," he said. The two other men lifted their brandies too, so Frankie followed suit, though she was puzzled Sergei had called poor little Marco a brat. After clinking their glasses together, they all drank to the absent brother.

"Why do you call Marco a brat?" she asked.

Sergei gave her a slow, wicked smile. "It does not mean what you think, beautiful Frankie. It is Russian for brother. I am Russian by birth."

"Sergei was brought to us all the way from Moscow by gypsies," Dimitri volunteered.

"Part of the way, *brat*, only part of the way from the

Ukraine border. Emilian and his Romani family should be passing by the island before winter sets in. We have never lost touch."

Frankie's eyes widened as she listened. "That's quite a story."

"We were all extremely lucky to come together under the care of our adoptive parents, Ian and Drusilla Brodie Stewart," Nik commented. "They were devoted to us four small, abandoned boys. We are the men we are today because of their love and support."

"*Mama kai o Bampas.*" Dimitri raised his glass, and the rest of the table followed his lead before drinking.

"*Yamas,*" Nik said, raising his glass once more. "To *our* health. And to our new venture."

"*Yamas!*" Frankie and the two other brothers repeated.

She stole a glance at Nik under her lashes. She felt so different now to how they and she had been even just a couple of weeks ago. It was hard to believe. The friction and the hard talk between them were gone. Working with him was comfortable and fun. He was even keen to have her meet his brothers and his friends. Every minute she'd spent with him since they'd agreed to be partners had been simply exhilarating, and the sex they were having mind-blowing...though it wasn't just sex; despite the terms of their union, it felt like making love, and she was a little scared to admit to herself that he had a part of her heart already. Though it wasn't part of her plan, it would be so easy to fall for him completely. It—she and him—was all moving so fast.

Chapter Twelve

WHEN THEY WALKED up the short path to the front door of Kostas's small house, which sat high on the mountainside beneath the village of Skalos, Até began straining on her leash. It was as if the dog knew she was coming home. Nik rapped the door knocker. Excited, high-pitched cries came from inside the house, and then the door was slowly pulled open. Theo peeped around it, his big brown eyes dancing with expectation, with Kostas standing behind him. Até let out a bark.

"*Chairete*!" As Theo hugged his dog, Nik and Kostas embraced, and then Kostas shook Frankie's hand.

They made their way to the back of the house, where there was a veranda. Kostas's mother served coffee and honey-and-nut pastries as they settled themselves down at a long, wooden table covered with a cloth. Theo took Até into the small, sheltered garden beyond set into the mountainside, now almost beside himself with joy that his new pet was finally with him; her arrival had been delayed by almost three weeks because he had been ill with tonsillitis.

Kostas squeezed Frankie's hand. "Thank you for making

my son very happy," he said in halting English.

Frankie squeezed back. "You are most welcome," she replied. "When will you be taking Até on the fire truck?"

Nik translated for her, and Kostas's face lit up with a big smile. "*Mama,*" he called out, and after a minute or two, his mother, Crysanthe, appeared, with what looked like a knitted tube. The older lady held it up and rotated it, and Frankie realised it was a little hand-made dog jacket, with buttons on the underside and an appliqued motif of the Hellenic Fire Service on the back.

Kostas said something in Greek. "His mother knitted it for Até to wear in the winter. It can get cold in the truck when we are up here on the mountain," Nik explained.

Frankie started laughing. "It's so cute!" She looked enquiringly at Kostas and his mum. "So it's okay for us to take Theo and Até to the beach for the rest of the afternoon? Theo is feeling better?"

Nik nodded. "Yes. We'll go to Trapazakia as planned."

After finishing their coffee and cakes, as they rose to leave, Kostas gestured to Nik that he wanted to speak in private. The men headed into the house, leaving Frankie to round up Theo and the dog. When they emerged again, she noticed Nik looking very serious.

"Is everything okay?" she asked once they were installed in the four-wheel drive and on their way, Theo strapped into a rear seat and singing softly to himself, and Até tethered quietly in the luggage area. Nik hadn't spoken since they'd left Kostas's house.

A muscle flexed in his jaw as he kept his eyes on the road. "I've had some news. But not in front of Theo. I will tell you when we get to the beach."

"Okay," Frankie agreed, wondering what could have changed his mood so dramatically.

They drove to a cove just along from Trapazakia's rocky harbour, where pine trees bordered white sand and small waves broke onto the shore. Even though it was almost the end of July, there were hardly any people about. Once they'd been unstrapped, Theo and Até bundled out of the car and rushed down onto the beach to play.

"It's beautiful here," Frankie commented, standing at the top of the wooden steps that led to the beach, pushing strands of hair that had been whipped up by the sea breeze away from her face. She turned around to Nik who was standing behind her. "So quiet and peaceful."

"Trapazakia is a well-kept secret. Not many vacationers know about it, even though it is so near to Agia Kalamaros."

Glad that she'd got him back and talking again, she dived in to keep the conversation going. "I read in a guide book that the village has a festival every year around Christmas?"

"Yes, on January the sixth, which is when we Greeks celebrate Christmas in the Orthodox church. The festival of St. Nikolaus takes place at the harbour. He is the patron of fishermen and sailors. It is quite a spectacle and a big celebration. All the crafts in the harbour are decorated with blue and white lights, and a priest blesses them, asking St. Nikolaus to watch over each one. The church's bell is rung and a cross is thrown into the sea, along with icons and flowers. I used to come every year with my parents and brothers…" He trailed off and looked at her with haunted eyes.

"Are you thinking of Marco?" she suggested gently after a minute or so.

"Yes. You said Alison told you what happened?"

She nodded.

He leaned forward and put his hands on her shoulders. "Come with me to walk along the beach. We can talk some more."

Once they were on the sand, she stopped and stepped away from him to take off her newly purchased sandals, and then held them up by their straps. "Flip-flops would have been better, but now I'm ready to walk," she pronounced wryly. But her attempt at a self-deprecating joke failed to raise a smile. His expression grave, he took her hand and they set off along the shore.

The sand felt warm and soft beneath her toes. They walked for some way, Theo and Até running in front of them. "Shall we sit here?" Nik suggested, pointing to some flat rocks worn smooth by endless tides. He called out in Greek to Theo, who settled himself with the dog nearby.

Frankie sank down beside Nik, allowing him to pull her to him before wrapping an arm around her. It felt warm, close, and natural. She leaned into him some more, and his grasp around her shoulders tightened. It made her realise how much she'd missed having a strong man by her side. "You said you had some news?" she probed softly.

He looked over to where Theo and Até were digging a hole, checking, she guessed, that the boy was out of earshot. A slight feeling of apprehension landed on her chest. What was it that Kostas had said to him?

"As you know, I was supposed to return to Paragolis tomorrow." His gaze went to the sea. "But I will be staying in Agia Kalamaros for the next few days now." He sighed heavily. "Kostas has told me that bones have been found up on the mountain. It is thought they are human…the bones of a child."

Frankie immediately grasped what he was saying. She swallowed her shock. "You think it's Marco? Oh, Nik."

His hand went up to her hair, and he began stroking it as if he needed to touch something. "It is possible. The police are to begin a further excavation at the site of the discovery tomorrow. They have asked for the fire brigade's help. I will be joining the dig."

She hesitated. "Do you think you should? Won't…won't it be terribly distressing if…"

His fingers stilled. "I need to be there," he gritted. "If it is Marco, I must be there." His hand fell away from her.

"I see. Is there anything I can do to help?"

He looked down at the sand. "No, it is okay, *pethi mou.*

So long as I am there for him." His head came up again. "It was my fault that Marco was taken," he said suddenly in a monotone.

She wrinkled her brow. "What do you mean? How could it have been your fault?"

"I was supposed to be watching him when he disappeared at the festival. Our parents had left him with me while they went with Dimitri and Sergei to get us all something to eat. But I was more interested in flirting with a girl. When I turned around, he had gone."

Frankie leaned her head against his shoulder and tried to wrap her arms around him. His body was rigid. "Nik…you can't blame yourself. How old were you when it happened? Fourteen? Little more than a child yourself."

"My parents had entrusted him to my care, and I failed to look after him." His voice cracked with emotion. "Because I was more interested in myself. I have lived with it ever since."

Frankie didn't know what to say. She rubbed his back and they sat without speaking, the silence broken only by the sounds of waves breaking and Theo chattering to Até.

After a while, Nik roused himself, looked at his watch, and spoke. "We had better take Theo and Até home now."

"All right." Frankie took her arm away from him and pushed herself off the rock. "I'll go and get them." She walked over to where the boy and the dog were still burrowing in the sand. When she'd got them going, she caught sight of Nik standing and staring sightlessly out to sea. She'd had no idea he was carrying such a burden of guilt.

"THERE IS ENOUGH food here to feed an army," Ali commented as she finished wrapping the last of the cold meat and cheese. "Have we got those bottles of water?"

"Yup." Frankie heaved up the giant cooler box. "We'd better start loading up." They had volunteered to take food and drink up to the team digging on the mountain today.

Ali came across with her carrier and grabbed one side of the cooler box handle. "Here, let me help you carry that. It's heavy."

"Bye, Gladys," she called out to the older lady who stood in the doorway of the shelter as they walked across the yard to the Land Rover.

They trundled up the winding road to the site of the dig. It was boiling hot, and Frankie could feel perspiration running down her spine. They pulled up in a lay-by at the side of the road. Beneath them, an area had been sealed off with tape and a tent had been erected on a rocky slope between scrubby bushes and trees. A policeman stood guarding the area. The team had been excavating the area for two days now. A shiver of apprehension ran through her. Could the remains of that poor little child really be down there?

She caught sight of Kostas and waved to him to come up. The man signalled he'd seen her, and he and another fireman came scrambling along the hillside. Giving their thanks, they took the cooler and the food and made their way back down.

"I wish I could go with them, do something," Frankie said, chewing her lip. "I feel so useless."

Ali shook her head. "They won't let you near, love. We need to let them get on with it." She patted Frankie's shoulder.

"Yes, I suppose so."

Ali gave her a shrewd look. "Maybe Nik will need you later."

"Maybe." Frankie exhaled her frustration and surveyed the scene below them again. A familiar figure emerged from the tent: Nik. He stopped, whipped his sweat-drenched T-shirt over his head, wiped his face with it, and accepted a bottle from Kostas. He opened the water and gulped it down. Even from this distance, she could see the muscles in his naked, glistening torso rippling as he moved. She longed to run down and comfort him.

That evening, she texted him to ask how he was and how things were going, but got no reply. The following day passed without news. After dinner, she went over to the shelter to shut it up for the night, trying to ignore the sinking feeling she had inside. Once the animals were dealt with and bedded down, she decided she could do with some air, so after locking the shelter door, she headed off across the yard and around the side of the house to the where Ali's small sheltered patio area lay. As she sat under there, the August twilight peeping through the creepers and vines climbing around her, one of the cats emerged from the vegetable garden and leapt onto her lap. Stroking Nyx's tabby fur, she allowed herself to think properly about Nik. Was she getting in too deep with him? It had been little more than a fortnight since they had hooked up, and here she was, already feeling involved, wanting to be close to him while he was suffering, just wanting him too much. That wasn't what she'd signed up for, was it? What had happened to her notions of a business arrangement and staying detached? She ought to put the brakes on and keep a hold of what she still had of her heart.

Her phone rang. She reached for it and looked at the screen. She hesitated for a couple more rings, and then answered. "Hi, Nik. Everything okay?"

"Can you come over, *pethi mou*? I need you."

I need you. The words tugged right at her soul. There was a pause while she wrestled with herself. "All right. Give me half an hour." She ended the call, knowing there was no turning back; she had taken another step further into the deep.

Forty minutes later, she was showered, changed, and standing at the gates to his house; there'd been no time to do her hair or makeup. She pressed the intercom. He greeted her at the door wearing a towelling robe, his hair clumped and clearly damp from a shower too. He looked unshaven and exhausted.

"Hey," she whispered, then stepped forward and hugged him.

His arms crept around her as he buried his face in her hair. When they finally let go of one another, he said, "Thank you for coming. I didn't want to be alone tonight."

She lifted her head. "Is…is it bad news?"

He grimaced. "If you mean, have we found Marco's remains, then no, I do not think so. We uncovered a skull, but it looks too big to be his. He was only two when he disappeared. The forensic expert thinks the skull and bones belonged to a child of about seven or eight, but tests will prove that for sure. We just have to wait to hear."

She digested this gruesome summary. "So that's good, isn't it? It means…that Marco could still be alive."

His smile was bitter. "You can look at it that way. Or presume he is somewhere else dead, and we might never know what happened to him, go on wondering and waiting."

"I'm—mmm…" She started to apologise for her tactless optimism, but he silenced her with his mouth, pulling her into the house and pressing her up against the wall. She felt his fingers go to the buttons that ran up the front of the bodice of her dress, deftly undoing them, before pushing the material apart to expose her braless breasts. He pulled his mouth away from hers and trailed his fingertips over her erect nipples, making her take a sharp intake of breath. His eyes flicked up to hers, and he held her mesmerised while he left her breasts to lift up her skirt and slide his hand inside her panties, seeking her core and stroking it. She groaned and parted her legs further, longing for him to enter her with his fingers. But he just kept stroking her rhythmically, making her slick with moisture, holding her gaze with a fierce intensity.

Driven nearly crazy with need, she pushed him and his hand from her. He took her cue and stepped back while she freed herself from her dress and underwear, then stood naked in front of him. He responded by unwrapping the tie of his robe and shrugging the garment off, then stepping forward again. She reached greedily for his erection, but he brushed her away, instead capturing her hips. "Ride me," he whispered, slamming her back against the wall, then deftly lifted her onto him, wrapping her legs around him, and thrust into her. Her climax was swift, pumping him until he shuddered his release too, and they collapsed against one another, panting. She brushed her lips against his chest. *In too deep.* The words echoed in her head, taunting her, but she knew she couldn't climb out again now, even if she was able to… It felt like she was falling in love.

Chapter Thirteen

NIK EMERGED FROM his lawyer's office in Paragolis, feeling pleased with the progress that had been made. The owner of the Villa Lemoni was wanting a quick sale and had been helpful in providing the information needed; the title deed had been obtained and the searches done. Now they would move on and get a final contract of purchase drawn up by a notary, who would also witness his and Frankie's signatures and deal with any registration and tax issues.

He had planned to return to Agia Kalamaros tonight. But he was seized by the impulse to drive there now and catch up with Frankie, persuade her to leave her duties at KATS and have lunch with him. As he drove over the mountain, he thought again about Marco. The dig for the child's remains had been tough and had stirred up the pain and guilt of his baby brother's disappearance all over again, but it was looking unlikely that the bones discovered had belonged to him. It was a matter of waiting for the forensic results from Athens, which would be through in a few weeks. Maybe Frankie was right—maybe Marco was out there somewhere. He didn't know what he believed; only that he would never stop hurting over Marco's loss.

He brightened when he pictured Frankie. Buying and making plans for the renovation of the Villa Lemoni had added a stimulating new dimension to his business affairs, which made him smile because that hadn't been a vital consideration for him when he'd made his proposition to her. *She* had been his goal. Of course, he'd got what he'd wanted on that score; making love to her was just as incredible and satisfying as he'd imagined it would be, and he couldn't have enough of her in bed. But the really unexpected development had been their increasing closeness as professional partners and friends. He had discovered just how smart, spirited, and funny she was, and he appreciated how sensitive and supportive she'd been about the discovery of the bones. He realised now what had been missing in his previous liaisons, why he had grown tired of those passing encounters. Perhaps once the Villa Lemoni was renovated and sold, they could take on another property and their sexual relationship could continue. He would be content with that.

He briefly considered pulling over to call her and let her know he'd be coming by, but then decided against it. He was less than a mile from Agia Kalamaros; from here, he could see the terracotta roofs and white walls of the village tumbling down the mountainside to the sea. He would surprise her.

He nosed the Spider along the road to KATS and turned into the yard. He noticed there was a hire car already parked next to the Land Rover. Tourists come to visit? He looked at his watch. It was before noon and outside visiting hours. Perhaps it was a special arrangement. He hoped it wouldn't stop Frankie from taking a break.

He walked up to the entrance and peered into the reception room. Nothing could have prepared him for what he saw. Frankie stood in the arms of a blond-haired man, her eyes closed and her palms against his chest as he kissed her on the lips...

"I HOPE I am not interrupting anything?"

The familiar, sardonic male voice had her eyes flying open and pulling away from Andrew. "Nik!" She took a couple of steps forward, then stopped, her heart thumping when she saw the cold anger freezing his expression. She gestured towards the other man stood behind her. "This...this is Andrew...my husband."

Nik nodded. "Your husband? My apologies for interrupting your...*reunion*."

"It's not what you think—"

"I think it is what I see. I will be in touch about the villa." He turned abruptly on his heel and walked out.

NIK SAT UNDER the pergola alongside the pool, nursing a Metaxa. He picked up his phone from the table and looked at the missed calls from Frankie. She'd tried four times to contact him since this morning, but he hadn't picked up. What was there to say? He'd found her in the arms of her husband, and, suddenly, those words she had uttered right after they had first slept together had come back to haunt him: *'I'm loving him less and less as each day passes'*. Less, but clearly she hadn't stopped loving the man entirely. No wonder she hadn't wanted to discuss her marriage. He would talk to her eventually because he had to, about the Villa Lemoni. But right now, he had no appetite for hearing her tell him that she was sorry but she had changed her mind and decided to rekindle her vows.

He took a swig of his brandy to rid his mouth of the bitter taste there. He stared into what remained of the dark-amber liquid in the glass and his thoughts darkened, old demons rushing back to join him. What had been that favourite saying of Monique, the French girl with whom he'd had a brief thing a couple of summers ago? *Plus ça change, plus c'est la même chose. The more it changes, the more it's the same thing*. How right that was. People he'd loved had been taken from him. His birth parents, his adoptive parents, Marco, Natassia, his best friend, Christos… Not that he was in love with Frankie, but he'd begun to care for her in a way he hadn't allowed himself to for a woman for many years. A self-deprecating smile played around his lips. It was ironic that, only hours earlier, he had been thinking about how there might be more for them after the villa was sold. But he'd been deceiving himself. Long-term relationships were not for him. Better that he returned to his old lifestyle of no involvement and no risk.

The buzzing of the intercom from inside the house broke into his brooding. Aspasia had gone home over an hour ago, so he would have to answer it. He attempted to ignore it. But, after a few seconds, it began sounding insistently again.

He downed the last of the Metaxa, and, reluctantly, he got up and went to the keypad in the hall. He could see Frankie on the mini video screen. Despite the graininess of the image, the distress on her features was visible. He decided to let her in. He would have to see her at some point, and he might as well get it over with.

When he opened the front door, he was greeted by her tear-streaked face. He schooled himself to remain impassive and stood to one side, gesturing for her to enter.

"Nik—"

"Go through to the patio," he said abruptly. "We can talk there. Would you like a drink?"

"No… yes. Just some water, thank you."

When he arrived with her glass, he found her perched on the edge of her seat, chewing her lip in that way he knew so well. She rubbed the heel of her hand against her damp eyes.

"Nik, you need to listen to me—" she started.

He placed the water on the table. He was not in the mood for sob stories. "What more is there to say, *pethi mou*? You have decided to get back with your husband."

"No, I haven't!"

He didn't react to her protest but sat down and surveyed her unemotionally. "You were in his arms and he was kissing you." He shrugged. "But if there is a chance to repair your marriage, I guess you should take it."

She sank back in her chair and shut her eyes in a frustrated motion. "No! You've got it all wrong."

"I do not think I have. I know what I saw. We agreed that we would be exclusive to one another while we have our arrangement."

Her lids flew open, and she put her palms together in a begging motion. "I know we did, and that hasn't changed. *Please* let me explain. I have no desire whatsoever to get back with Andrew. I was as shocked as you to see him. He turned up this morning without warning. But he didn't want a reunion; he'd come to say to say goodbye."

Nik raised an eyebrow. "Goodbye?"

"Yes, because the divorce will be finalised soon."

He felt a leap of relief, but that was almost instantly dispelled by the persistent memory of her in her husband's arms. "If that is so, why did I see him kissing you?"

Her features creased up. "Oh, Nik, I can understand how it must have looked when you came upon us like that. But believe me when I tell you that it wasn't anything dodgy—just two people who'd shared a past letting go. He only pecked me on the lips, and that was after he apologised for what he'd put me through." She clasped her hands together. "You know, I'm glad he came here and did that. I've had some difficult times since we split up, and it helped me to have heard him say sorry. In fact, I think that, in time, we may even be able to be friends."

Nik couldn't hide his puzzlement. "Friends? With this man who has betrayed you?"

She smiled. "Okay, so maybe it won't happen immediately. But my instinct has always been that it's healthier to forgive, even if you don't forget. I don't want to become bitter and twisted—and I nearly did, you know. But I think I've reached a place where I can be civil with him and his girlfriend now, and, in time, perhaps I will forgive. It's for the best." She tilted her head on one side thoughtfully. "I'm looking forward to getting my financial settlement. I can put in a court order for it to happen once the divorce has been granted. Apparently, I can do that from here, with no need to return to England, which I prefer. And the quicker that happens, the quicker I can pay you back for the Villa Lemoni."

He sensed himself bristle a little. "I thought we had also agreed you would not pay me back?"

He noticed that she raised her chin slightly and, if he wasn't mistaken, a little defiantly, before she replied. "Well, it was very kind of you to offer to waive repayment and let me take the profit from the resale. But I can't accept all of that from you. It's too much. I've always planned to pay you back eventually."

Why did that sound like a rejection? Feel like a barrier that she was keeping erected between them, and just when he'd begun to anticipate they might get closer? The vision of her in the arms of the other man whose lips had been against hers hovered in his mind once again and stung at him like an angry wasp. She might be getting divorced, but had she really stopped caring for her husband? Her *friend*?

"Say something, Nik. We are okay still, aren't we? You know I'm not a liar or a cheat."

He mentally shook himself. He refocused and saw her blue eyes were wide and pleading. "*Nai*, we are okay, *oraiotatos mou*," her responded almost mechanically. He rose up and walked around the table, halting behind her and bending to kiss the side of her neck, inhaling the fresh scent of her. But it wasn't okay. A distrusting voice nagged at him now, after what he had witnessed and heard today. However, he also realised his driving need for her and her body couldn't be pushed aside; it gripped him more strongly and tightly than ever. For now, he had to continue with getting his fill of her, get her out of his system. It was a risky strategy when they were legally bound together over the villa, but he would let time be the decider if her intentions were really true.

Chapter Fourteen

FRANKIE LAY IN bed facing Nik. He'd made love to her tonight, and the previous few nights, with an intense passion, like he wanted their bodies to fuse into one, leaving her sated and her senses thrumming. Physically, she knew she had all of him. But emotionally? It niggled at her that she'd been feeling a distance very recently—that somehow a gulf had opened up between them. She perceived it had started after he'd seen her with Andrew. But she explained what had happened, and he'd assured her that they were okay. Or was it because she'd told him she would be paying him back for the villa when she could manage it? Had she hurt his pride? Then the memory of Ali talking about Natassia, his ex-fiancee, and how she'd jilted him and put him off commitment, crowded in with the rest of her doubts. She'd wondered quite a lot about Natassia since and had been waiting for the right moment to broach the subject with him. Perhaps that was making him wary when they were getting closer fast?

Her head rattled with all the possibilities. Maybe she was overthinking everything, and he was on edge simply because he needed to hear the results of the forensic tests on the skull and bones. Though the police were assuming they belonged to an older child, until that was proven, she could imagine how unsettled he must be feeling.

She reached out a finger to stroke his cheek. "Hey, what are you thinking?"

He turned his head on the pillow and gazed at her with hooded eyes. "How beautiful you are, *pethi mou.* How perfect it is to make love to you."

"That's because it's perfect making love to you." Her finger trailed down to his chest, and she swirled it in the hair there. "But you seem preoccupied these days. Is it because of Marco?" she asked, hoping he would confirm that and dispel her other fears.

She felt his chest heave as he took in a deep breath. "He is in my thoughts, yes."

She moved closer and snuggled up to him, feeling relieved and hoping to get him to open up some more. There was a lot she didn't know. "I'd love to understand more about him, if you want to tell," she said gently. "About how you and he, and Dimitri and Sergei, came to be adopted by Ian and Drusilla. Do you know anything about your birth parents or your brothers'?"

"Okay." He curled his bronzed arms around her. "As you know, I am the oldest. My birth parents lived in Agia Kalamaros, but they were killed in an earthquake—"

"Earthquake?" Frankie raised her head to look at him in

surprise. "Oh, my goodness, I'm so sorry. I had no idea you were orphaned. Or that there are earthquakes in Greece."

"Yes, *agapimeni mou*, there are. In the case of Kathos, a fault line runs just east of the island, where the European and Ionian tectonic plates meet. Have you ever noticed that many of the buildings in the village, though they are in the traditional style, are of modern construction?"

She pursed her lips thoughtfully. "Now you come to mention it, yes. Though Ali and Pavlos's place is old, and so is this house."

"Not every building was destroyed in the earthquake, but many of the smaller, more simply built houses simply crumbled and many people were killed. My parents and my older brother all perished, but I was found alive in the ruins, still in my crib. Some of my father's relatives survived too, but they immigrated to America after the quake, leaving me in the orphanage in Paragolis. Ian and Drusilla had not been able to have children, and when they heard about me through the local priest, they applied to adopt."

"Wow, that's really something. And what about Dimitri and Sergei? How did Sergei get from Russia to here?" She snuggled back against him and he held her tighter; this was the kind of closeness with him she adored.

"Their backgrounds are even more dramatic and heart-breaking than mine. Dimitrios will not mind me telling you that he was the son of a prostitute. She was originally from Agia Kalamaros, but lived in Paragolis near the docks.

Dimitri thinks his father may have been an Italian sailor."

"Goodness me. So why did his mother give him up? Or was he taken away from her?"

"She was murdered. He was found in her apartment, clinging to her body. He was two years old, and she had been dead for three days."

Frankie gasped. "Oh, Nik, that's awful. Poor Dimitri. So how did he come to Ian and Drusilla?"

"His mother's family, who lived here in the village, didn't want him because of how he'd been conceived. So the priest stepped in again and arranged the adoption through the church."

She lay still for a few minutes, processing the deeply heart-rending circumstances that had brought Nik and the oldest of his brothers to their loving family. "Do you or Dimitri keep in touch with your surviving relatives?" she asked after a short while. "Or have those ties been broken?"

"I have travelled to America and been reunited with my uncles and cousins. And Dimitri is now reconciled with his maternal aunt. It helped that both of us have made money," he added sardonically.

"I bet it did. And how about Sergei?" she prompted softly.

"Sergei's journey to us was incredible. He was born in Moscow. His father was a soldier in the Red Army. After his father abandoned his mother, she became an alcoholic. The only loving influence in his life was his grandmother, but she died when he was eight, and he ran away, using money she had given him to buy a train ticket. Nobody noticed a small boy travelling alone, because everything was in turmoil after the Soviet Union had collapsed the year before. He went to the Ukrainian border and sneaked into Romania, where he was picked up by gypsies. He stayed with them until they got down here to Greece. But when they moved on, he was left behind on Kathos and fended for himself, until Ian found him living on a beach and brought him home. It took a long time and a lot of wrangling with the Greek and Russian authorities for him to be adopted. His mother demanded money for him."

"That *is* incredible. Ian and Drusilla must have been amazing people."

"They were. It cannot have been easy, bringing up three small boys from disparate difficult backgrounds. But they gave us so much love. We have all turned out okay, I think. Like many on this island, Dimitri has made a fortune from growing olives and selling their oil to the Italians, who then export it to the rest of the world, and Sergei is a successful music producer in Athens."

"You certainly have." She smiled, loving being in his arms and hearing him talk about his family history. She hesitated before asking, "Am I right in thinking that Marco was adopted by Ian and Drusilla as well?"

"You are. Almost twenty-two years ago in late December, an Italian girl arrived in Agia Kalamaros. She was a young teenager and pregnant. She gave birth alone to a boy and abandoned him on the steps of the church. The only clue to the baby's origins was that he was wrapped in a plastic bag that carried the address of a grocery store in the port of Bari in southern Italy, from where ferries sail to Paragolis. The priest turned to Ian and Drusilla, who took him in as their fourth son and named him Marco."

"He was with you for two years?"

"Yes."

Hearing the heavier, emotional note that had entered his voice, she stopped her questioning and just let him be, not wanting to cause him more distress. She listened to his breathing even out as he settled into a doze, and pondered on what he'd told her tonight. Though he'd obviously had a wonderful, loving home with Ian and Drusilla, as had the other boys, what must it have been like for him growing up knowing his real parents had been killed, and that his relatives didn't want him? Or for Dimitri and Sergei, one orphaned by violence, the other rejected by his birth mother and forced to wander through Russia and the Balkans at such a young age? And then they'd had to deal with Marco's disappearance, and now the question that hung over the remains on the mountain. She shivered. Definitely, she could understand if Nik had baggage, as Ali had called it. She remembered the glass of Metaxa for the missing brother that had sat across the table at *Artemis TZ*. It had been poignant and touching but also, she understood now, a symbol of the guilt she'd only recently realised Nik carried. If only she could help him to forgive himself for something she felt sure nobody could have prevented.

She felt him stir and stretch slightly. "Mmm…" He sighed and pecked a kiss on the top of her head. "Sorry, *pethi mou*, I feel asleep for a while."

"I could tell that by your snoring," she teased.

"I was *snoring*?" he queried huffily. "That cannot be right."

"How do you know?" she teased. "You were asleep."

"I know I do not snore."

"Okay." She giggled. "You weren't snoring. I was pulling your leg."

"Pulling my leg?" He looked down. "My leg is where it should be, and I do not see your hand on it."

"It means I was teasing you."

"Ah, okay. Another strange English expression." He smiled. "If you would like to put your hand on me now, I can show you exactly where to place it." He grabbed her fingers and guided them to his hardening arousal, then rolled over and positioned himself above her. "Make me ready for you," he growled, his eyes blazing.

FRANKIE DAWDLED IN the reception room of KATS, reliving the delicious lovemaking of the night before. Memories of

Nik's tongue, his touch, the feel of him inside her, the scent of his skin as it had moved against hers and the joy he'd given her, making her shudder with satisfaction, flooded her senses.

"What are you smiling to yourself about, missy?" Ali interrupted her pleasurable recollections.

"Uh? Oh, nothing," she denied as breezily as she could.

"It didn't look like nothing to me. If I didn't know any better, I would say you were thinking about Nik."

Frankie shrugged, unable to stop her smile getting wider. "Maybe."

Ali rubbed her arm affectionately. "It's love, isn't it?"

She felt a rush of emotion at the older woman's incisive question. "*No*," she defended, knowing her cheeks were flushing up and Ali wouldn't believe her. She sighed, but then admitted, "Well, not quite."

"But you're well on the way." Ali gave her a sideways hug. "I've seen how you light up when you see him or talk about him. Does he return your feelings?"

"I don't know." She sighed. "I have a wonderful time when I'm with him, and we've been getting on really well together when it comes to buying and making plans to renovate the Villa Lemoni. I'm really excited about that—"

"But?"

Her smile faded. "*But* recently, it feels like he's holding something back. When we first got together, he was totally present. Now, it's like there's a part of him that's withdrawn from me. I asked him whether he was feeling preoccupied by the pressure of waiting to hear whether those remains on the mountain belonged to Marco, and he sort of said yes."

"Perhaps. It'll be a dreadful thing to have to deal with if it's true. Let's hope it isn't." Ali regarded her, her expression perplexed. "It hasn't got something to do with the appearance of Andrew then?"

Frankie's brow creased, Ali's question causing her a little ripple of unease. "He accepted it when I explained Andrew had actually come to say goodbye. He said we were okay when I asked him afterwards. He hasn't mentioned it since, and I've got no appetite for talking about it or the divorce any more than I have to. I can't wait to put all that behind me." She sighed again. "No, I'm pretty sure it's to do with Marco. He's just having a hard time talking about it."

Ali nodded. "You're probably right. Whatever it is, I think you need to be patient with him, give him time. He hasn't actually had a long-term relationship for a quite a while, not since Natassia—"

"I had been wondering if that had something to do with it," Frankie interjected. "Will you tell me about her?"

Ali frowned. "You've not asked Nik yet?"

She shook her head.

"I would have preferred it if you'd talk to him. But I guess you need to know. They'd been together since their teens. Their wedding was organised and everything, and then she jilted him for his best friend, Christos."

"Nik, jilted? He can have any woman he wants!"

"It's hard to believe, isn't it? But it happened and he was totally cut up about it at the time. He lost the girl he loved and his friend from childhood, and he was betrayed by both of them."

"When was this?"

"About ten years ago. He would have been twenty-four." Ali gave her another squeeze. "Even love-gods suffer rejection. Like I say, give him time. I expect he's feeling as wary as you did a couple of months back."

"Okay," Frankie replied. She wondered how she could get Nik to talk more about Natassia without appearing gossipy or nosy. He held such a lot about his past inside himself. "That's good advice. Thanks for being such a great friend." She paused, and then grinned. "Changing the subject, I've had an idea about further fundraising for the shelter."

Ali's eyes lit up. "Oh, yes? That would be very welcome since the new boiler has taken all the donations that Nik and the fire station made."

"Why don't we have an open day here? It'll have to be in the next two or three weeks, because we want to catch the tourists before the season ends. I thought we could ask Nik and Kostas if one of the fire trucks could be brought up here for the kids. We could have Até and Theo too, and we could serve traditional English tea, homemade lemonade, and cakes for a small price."

"Oh, I see. Have I got to get baking, then?" Ali pulled a face.

"Well, you make the best cakes I've ever tasted. And I do believe Gladys isn't bad either. That fruit cake she brought in for us was yummy."

Ali laughed. "It was full of alcohol, I know that. I couldn't walk in a straight line after I'd eaten a slice." She clapped her hands together. "I like that idea very much. You get on to Nik and Kostas, and I'll rope in Gladys, and ask Sally to order in what we need in the way of ingredients and tea and put up posters in the mini-market. Maybe Nik can display a couple in *Artemis AK*, and persuade a few other bar and restaurant owners on the strip to do the same."

Frankie nodded her agreement. "Gladys's daughter and her husband and family are here for the week. I'll see if her grandchildren will help me post flyers in the hotels and holiday apartments. I'll also update the website. Gosh, we haven't got that much time to get it all organised. Think we're going to be busy!"

Chapter Fifteen

FRANKIE ADDED HER signature under Nik's and handed the document back to the notary. She straightened up. "So now we just have to exchange contracts and the Villa Lemoni will be ours?"

Nik stepped forward and slid his arm around her waist. "We are going to celebrate, *pethi mou*. I have booked a table for dinner this evening at the best restaurant in town." He turned to the notary. "*Efcharisto*. Thank you."

After they'd left the notary's office, Nik stopped. Placing a hand under her chin, he brushed a kiss across her lips. "I have to drop in at the club and deal with some paperwork. Take a taxi back to the apartment, serve yourself with a drink, and take a long, hot bath. I will see you there." His eyes burned with a raw intensity that she recognised well.

"Okay," she whispered, a need that matched his bubbling inside her. She watched him walk away across the square, his muscular body carrying his grey lightweight business suit with a sleek style that made other women turn and stare.

His penthouse apartment had a spectacular view of the

harbour at Paragolis and, further down the sound, of the docks where ferries, oil tankers, and containers sailed in and out. After obeying orders and taking a luxurious soak in its sunken whirlpool bath, surrounded by candles, her muscles relaxed by the power-jets of hot water, she'd fished her black jersey maxi dress from her overnight bag and changed for dinner. Now, she was standing on the roof terrace taking in the maritime scene. This was where Nik's brother, Dimitri, had started life. She swirled the ice cubes in her drink. It would be good to have a quiet, intimate dinner this evening, certainly to celebrate the purchase of the Villa Lemoni, but also because she wanted to tell Nik she was going to have to take a short trip back to the UK next week that she'd not anticipated, to sort out the sale of her partnership in the estate agency with Andrew. She really didn't want to go, but the prospect that everything would be settled once and for all, and at the same time, she could retrieve some clothes and possessions to be shipped back to Kathos, had persuaded her she should. She also had an opportunity for marketing the villa to prospective British buyers once it had been refurbished through Andrew's new agency—she was sure Nik would be pleased by what was on offer.

"Turtles swim in the harbour. Perhaps we will see them later." He surprised her by coming up behind her and started nuzzling her neck, making her body leap in response. "You look and smell delicious, *agape mou*." His hands came up to cup her breasts. She wasn't wearing a bra. As his thumbs began caressing her nipples, they hardened and thrust against the thin material of her dress, desire for him infusing her belly. A small moan escaped her.

"Do you want to eat now or make love?" he asked softly. "They will hold the table for us."

"Make love." She rotated in his arms and felt his arousal press into her. "*Now.*" His mouth slammed down on hers, ravishing it.

Afterwards, as they walked hand in hand to a waterside taverna, she still vibrated from his fierce possession of her, when he had taken her from behind, pushing into her with hard thrusts, bringing both of them quickly into breathless, shattering climaxes. She wished they could skip dinner and just go to bed and spend the rest of the night in one another's arms instead. She shot him a discreet sideways glance. Their physical need for one another was incredible, insatiable. But did he know that her feelings for him were growing stronger by the day too? Recently, in quiet moments, she'd begun to dream about a future with him, beyond working on the Villa Lemoni. That, in time, they might settle down together, and what it would be like to have his baby... She vigorously wiped away the fantasies from her mind, like she always did. What was the point of letting such notions run wild? He was Nik. He continued to hold back emotionally. He wanted her in his bed, but not forever in his life.

A few minutes later, they were seated by the taverna's attentive owner at a secluded table on a private side-deck and being offered a traditional Greek dinner menu: marinated eggplant with mint and goat's cheese accompanied by olive, lemon, and thyme and rosemary flatbread for their starter, leg of lamb with garlic and rosemary for the main course—served with roasted garbanzo beans, Swiss chard and potatoes with lemon vinaigrette—and sticky chocolate baklava to finish.

She gave him a saucy look from under her lashes as she set about her dessert. "The food here is amazing," she pronounced, licking her spoon. "I'm glad we had sex before we ate. I'm almost full to bursting."

A mellow smile curved his mouth. "Sex and food—the best combination. We will sleep well tonight." He laid down his own spoon and finished his wine. "How are the preparations for the open day at KATS coming along?"

She swallowed another mouthful of baklava, savouring its gooey sweetness. "Okay so far. Thank you for helping with getting the posters displayed."

He raised a hand. "You are welcome. I spoke to Kostas, and you will have a fire truck and a couple of crew. Theo and Até are getting very excited about being there too."

She beamed. "That's brilliant. It's all coming together." She hesitated. This was a good opportunity to bring up her trip. "Though it's going to be a bit of a race to get everything done before I fly to the UK at the weekend. Ali and Gladys will have to deal with the last-minute stuff."

"To the UK? And why are you planning to go there all of

a sudden, *pethi mou*?"

"That's what I wanted to talk to you about. Andrew has found someone who wants to partner with him in our estate agency and buy out my share. It will make things much easier if I travel to England and spend next week there getting everything handed over and the legal papers signed and sealed. I can also arrange for some of my stuff that has been sitting in my parents' loft to be sent over here."

He raised an eyebrow. "So you *are* planning on returning to Kathos?"

She felt her skin prickle a little. Why had his tone turned *mocking*? "Yes, of course. It's just a week's trip to sort out my life, and then I'll be back here ready for the open day, and also to start work on the villa. We'll need to have it finished by the end of the year if we are to get it on the market to sell. We want to catch prospective buyers who want it as a holiday home and ready to move into by next spring. Actually, with regard to selling, Andrew will advertise it to British clients through his agency—"

"You have asked *your husband* to sell our villa?" Nik cut in, his expression tense now.

"No, he's offered to do it…and I feel it's a good move. It makes sense to try as many avenues as possible, and I think there will be people who'll be interested in a Mediterranean retreat where they can away from the rainy weather back home. I can get it organised next week. We can put it on here with a local agent as well," she added hurriedly when she saw his brows draw together and his face darken.

He rubbed his chin, his stubble making a rasping sound against his fingers. "I thought we were partners, Frankie. Did it not occur to you to consult me first before you and your husband discussed this?"

She chewed her lip. "I thought you trusted me to take care of the property sales side. That's part of my role, isn't that what we agreed? I do the interior design and work with the builders, and then I get it sold. You are the investor and line up all the services and deal with the legal stuff."

"We did indeed agree that, *agapimeni mou.* But I presumed you would discuss important decisions such as this with me first, and I do not remember agreeing to include your *husband* in our deal." His gaze on her narrowed as he asked coolly, "If he sells the villa, he will be receiving a commission, I presume?"

"No, and that's the most appealing aspect. He's said he'll do it for free. And remember, he'll soon be my ex-husband."

Nik leaned back in his chair, rapping out an impatient beat on its arm. "But still your *friend.*" He bit out that last word. "So you and your soon-to-be ex-husband have this all sewn up between you?"

She felt a flush rise up her neck, perplexed and hurt as to why her good intentions were being misunderstood. "It isn't like that. You're making it sound all underhand and sneaky! I was just trying to do my best to market the property when it's ready, and the fact I can have it done for no fee—"

"But why did you not consult me first? Why keep it a secret?"

"I haven't kept a secret! You said you trusted me to deal with the sale of the property, and I'm telling you about it now. If you really object, I can cancel it."

She could see something fierce burning in his eyes. He turned and signalled to the waiter to bring the bill. He reached inside his jacket, which was hanging on the back of his chair, and withdrew his wallet and credit card. "I find it hard to understand why you would want to continue to stay in touch and do business with the man you are divorcing. Who cheated on you."

"Yes, he betrayed me with another woman, and that was devastating. You know that. But that never prejudiced me to the fact that he's as straight as a die when it comes to real estate and extremely good at sales and marketing."

"You are very forgiving of him and what he did to you."

Frankie could feel her hands balling into tight fists in her lap. She blew out a calming breath. "Actually, I have just about forgiven him. It's actually very empowering and helpful for moving on and letting go."

He shot her another searing look and turned to attend to the payment of the dinner bill. "But if you are still including him in our plans, then it would seem to me that you haven't moved on at all." He stood up abruptly. "It is getting late. We should go back to the apartment."

Frankie also rose and followed him out of the taverna,

temporarily rendered speechless by his obtuse statement. Why couldn't he understand that she was finally reaching an amicable end to her marriage, an outcome she was happy with? And that it had brought the opportunity of a smart commercial deal. Why couldn't he see that both outcomes were good for her and for him?

He took her arm, and they started walking along the brightly lit street. She could see from the set of his jaw that he was annoyed. "Why are you making such a fuss about this?" she demanded, finding her voice again. "What is your problem?"

He stopped in his tracks and faced her. "*My* problem?" he gritted. "Can you not see how this looks? I find you in the arms of your husband who you are supposed to be divorcing, and you tell me that you hope you will be friends with him. Then, without warning, you announce you are returning to him and allowing him to handle the sale of our joint property. Yet you tell me that your marriage to him is over and you have moved on. I do not think so!"

She shook herself free of his grip, emotion boiling up inside her. "Oh, for goodness' sake, Nik, it's not like that at all! You're putting the worst spin on it!"

"I am saying it as it appears to me, *pethi mou*. You appear unable to let go of him."

"Who are you to judge me about letting go?" she flared, emotion coursing through her and loosening her tongue. "*You* who refuse to commit to a woman because your fiancée dumped you ten bloody years ago? How is that letting go?" As soon as the angry words had flown out of her mouth, she wished she could take them back.

He looked briefly stricken, then took his hand away from her arm and started walking away at a fast pace.

"Wait!" she called after him, then pulled up the skirt of her long dress and began running after him. She caught up with him. "I'm sorry," she panted, "I shouldn't have said that—"

He kept walking and didn't look at her. "You have been listening to gossip again," he grated, "And you accuse me of judging you."

"Nik, I really am sorry. It was very wrong of me to say it."

By now, they had reached the main door to the apartment building. He hammered in the code to the entry keypad. She followed him inside, and they rode up in the lift without speaking. She leaned against the wall, her head reeling; how had everything blown up and got this out of control so quickly?

When they entered the apartment, he spun around and faced her, his expression like granite, stony and hard. "Go and pack your belongings. I will order a taxi to take you back to Agia Kalamaros."

"Nik, please! Let's talk. It's all a dreadful misunderstanding—"

He surveyed her with a black glare. "On the contrary, I

now understand everything." He inhaled. "It is over."

She stood for a moment feeling winded, as if she'd been punched. "Nik, no—"

He cut across her. "Everything is finished between us. I will have my lawyer transfer the title deed of the villa to me and cancel our agreement."

"You can't do that!" she responded, aghast.

"I can. After all, I am paying for it all."

"But I signed an agreement with you, which you have to honour!"

"So sue me," he invited.

She remained rooted to the spot, silent with shock, her heart pounding.

"I have nothing more to say to you. I will call that cab, and you can be on your way back to England. And your husband."

Chapter Sixteen

THE FRONT DOOR to Alison and Pavlos's house was open. Nik stepped out of the hot September sunshine into the cool stone-flagged hall and called out, "Alison! It is Nik."

As he waited for her to appear, the delicious aroma of baking teased his nostrils. He guessed she was preparing for the shelter's open day next week.

"Hi, Nik, come and join me." She came around a door and beckoned to him, and he followed her into the kitchen. "Come on, Hades, off you go." She tipped a chair next to the table to unseat a jet-black tomcat. He jumped off, his tail flicking with irritation. "Please sit down. Cup of tea?"

Nik nodded, settled himself down, and waited while she brought over a tray bearing a teapot, mugs and what looked like a platter of small cakes.

"I'd like you to try these for me," she requested, placing the platter on the tabletop. "Ginger, sultana, and spiced buns. I want to serve them at the open day, but I need you to taste test them first. Tell me if they need more ginger or spices."

"Thank you." He took the plate bearing a bun from her, and also accepted a mug of tea.

"I'm glad you came," she said. She sat down next to him and helped herself to a bun. "Look, I'm going to get straight to the point. You've known me for a long time, and that I say what I think. Frankie phoned me yesterday evening. Nik, she sounded so down. I'm worried about her. I understand she said and did things that upset you a great deal. But were they so bad that you had to cut ties with her completely?"

He concentrated on slicing his bun in half. When Alison had called him first thing this morning and invited him to tea, he'd realised she wanted to talk about his split with Frankie. He liked and respected Alison a great deal, so he'd agreed. "I appreciate you feel you must support Frankie, but it is over between us." He could hear his voice sounded stiff and cold, but that was how he felt about it now.

Alison looked perturbed. "Nik, really? It was going so well. You and she were getting going with your new property project, and it was clear to anyone who saw the two of you that there was something special developing between you."

The mention of 'something special' almost tripped him, but, within a moment, he had a grip on himself. "I had second thoughts about our collaboration."

"But you've only just exchanged contracts on the villa and everything. What made you pull back when you'd gone so far with it?" She put her head on one side, her brown eyes reminding him of a beady bird. "I hear you objected to

Andrew handling the marketing and selling in England."

There was no point in evading Alison's questions; she was a straight talker and liked a straight answer. "I felt it was unwise for her husband, whom she is divorcing, to deal with the Villa Lemoni."

"I have to say I also questioned the wisdom of using Andrew's services." Alison folded her arms and sighed. "It seems to me, after the way he's behaved to her, he's basically untrustworthy, and she'd be better putting him completely behind her. But it's in Frankie's nature to forgive, and her approach is that Andrew has always been a good estate agent, so if he is feeling guilty about what happened, she might as well turn it to her advantage."

Nik raised his eyebrows at this new information. "Guilty?"

Alison nodded. "Yes. She explained to me that she wanted to do the best she could to maximise the financial success of the villa project. When Andrew had his guilt trip and offered to market the villa in Britain, and not to take a fee if he sold it, she thought why not? It could be a smart move. She felt that, as an astute businessman, you would appreciate it too."

"My opinion was not asked for. I was presented with a *fait accompli.*" He averted his eyes and took a sip of his tea.

"But I thought you gave Frankie free rein to handle the sales and marketing side?"

"We agreed she would deal with those things, but I presumed she would discuss any major developments with me first."

Alison considered this for a few seconds. "Okay, I can see how you would want that. But I'm not sure Frankie understood that. Although, she did get to talk to you before returning to England, so there was an opportunity to veto it if you didn't agree."

He rubbed the back of his neck, feeling uncomfortable at her explanation. She'd made him appear ever so slightly unreasonable. But, he reminded himself, Frankie had said and done other things he wouldn't accept. Then his gaze was drawn over Alison's shoulder to a photo that was taped to the fridge. He hadn't noticed it until now. It was of Frankie, with her arms around Theo and Até. Her wide smile and her clear blue eyes reached out to him, and he was instantly reminded of her freshness—her skin, her golden hair, her clean scent. He swallowed hard. This past week had been hell trying to banish taunting thoughts of her, far from him in England and with her husband.

Alison picked up on the direction of his gaze. Unfolding her arms, she swivelled in her seat to look at the photo. She turned back to him. "You miss her, don't you?"

He tore his eyes away. He wanted to deny feeling anything, but no words came. As he struggled for a reply, Alison spoke again. "You're not jealous of Andrew, are you, Nik?"

Her forthright observation caught him by surprise. "Jealousy is an ugly emotion."

"I agree. If it's out of control, it can be destructive and ultimately self-defeating. But I'm of the opinion that a little jealousy can be a good thing if it motivates you to cherish and protect your relationship, realise how much you care for the other person." Her hand went to his shoulder. "Nik, listen. You're letting a wonderful woman slip through your fingers because of your stupid pride. Frankie told me how you found her and Andrew together when he came here to talk about the divorce. When you saw her with him…well, I get that it caused you to think you were being played false. But what you actually witnessed was two people who were married, then torn apart by infidelity, making their peace, not some great reunion. Believe me, though the impact on Frankie has been huge and it took her time to disentangle herself from her marriage and her emotions, she feels little for Andrew now. She's determined to be civilised, but she can't wait to divorce him."

He leaned back in his chair. *Stupid pride.* He felt the wasp's sting again, remembering that moment when he'd seen Frankie's husband kissing her. Alison meant well, but she hadn't seen what he had. "I know you care about Frankie a great deal, but it is too much of a coincidence." His tone hardened. "The embrace with her husband. Saying she hoped she'll be friends with her husband. This sudden trip to the UK to see him, and the plan to market the villa through him… She still has feelings for him, Alison!"

She pursed her lips "Nik, it's not as simple as that. How

can it be? She was married to Andrew for seven years. It'll take time for her to completely put the memories of that behind her. On the other hand, there's every reason for her to move on. For one thing, what about the baby Andrew and his partner Becky are expecting? Poor Frankie. This week, while she's been back in the UK, she's not only had to cope with seeing Becky face to face and pregnant, but Becky's also been flashing a new engagement ring as well."

His head lifted up, and he shot Alison a sideways glance. "Baby? Frankie's husband has made his girlfriend pregnant? I was not aware of this."

Alison's surprise was visible. "Oh! Frankie didn't tell you? Yes, Becky must be about five or six months along now." She hesitated as if she was considering saying more.

He exhaled heavily. This was a bombshell, in more ways than one. "I did not know about the baby, Alison."

The older woman gave him a curious look. "I see. I thought Frankie had explained. Well, maybe there's a reason for that, and maybe you need to hear it. It's been incredibly challenging for Frankie, knowing Becky is pregnant. She wanted a baby so much herself, and she was devastated when she discovered Becky was expecting Andrew's child. She's coming to terms with it now. Actually, I feel proud of her for being able to go back and deal civilly with both of them despite that, not to mention the engagement *and* the humiliation of them betraying her so badly."

He rubbed his face. "If I had known all of this..." He

trailed off as he toyed with the idea that maybe, because he hadn't known all the facts, he had come to the wrong conclusion. Now he had more pieces of the puzzle, he could understand there was little reason for Frankie to run after her husband, beyond getting what she could from him. He felt a sense of anger starting to rise in him on her behalf, coupled with the creep of self-reproach. Had he shot from the hip, let his brain migrate to his trousers again?

"Starting to reconsider?" Alison asked wryly.

He grimaced. "It does change things. If I had known," he repeated slowly, "I might have seen and done things differently."

She smiled at him encouragingly. "And what about Natassia? Can you forgive Frankie for what she said? She told me how you reacted." She drew in a deep breath. "She wasn't repeating gossip. It was me who told her about your failed engagement, because I was encouraging her to cut you some slack."

"Cut me some slack?"

"Give you some space and time as you haven't had a long-term relationship since you and Natassia split."

"Why would I need time and space? That was all in the past, finished long ago."

"But that's not true, is it?"

He studied what remained of his tea in his mug. "It was until Frankie stirred up that particular ghost to come back and haunt me," he murmured.

"Frankie shouldn't have said what she did, Nik, especially when you'd never talked to her about it yourself. But, all the same, she spoke the truth when she brought up Natassia, didn't she? She didn't stir up that ghost, because, in reality, it never left you. You haven't dealt with what happened to you ten years ago."

His head snapped up at the accusation. "That is very harsh, Alison."

"Oh, my love," she said, her voice becoming kinder, "I don't mean to be. I've known you since you were a small boy. I watched you grow up into a man. A very fine and successful man, who I know has a good heart, and who has so much to give a woman, if only you'll allow yourself to." She paused as he levelled his eyes on her. "You've lost more people who were dear to you than most, some of them in unimaginably painful ways. But take it from me, trying to ignore that pain isn't healthy. I remember that, years ago, after I'd suffered a succession of miscarriages and I was told by a specialist that I'd never be able to carry a baby to full term, I was paralysed with grief. But I found out that the only way to get over that grief was to face up to it."

He looked at her for long seconds, unable to mask his surprise, his anger extinguished. "I am so very sorry to hear that. It must have been extremely difficult for you and Pavlos."

"It was. But Pavlos is a wonderful husband who supported me and cried with me. We dealt with our losses together.

And I was able to fulfil myself by setting up the shelter. Now I have fur babies to nurture." She laughed, but quickly grew serious again. "I don't think you've allowed yourself to grieve, Nik, so you haven't healed and that's holding you back, even clouding your judgement. Let it out, share it, make your own particular peace with it, find new things to replace what you've lost. Don't blame Frankie."

He absorbed Alison's advice and sat silently for a few minutes while he tried to unwind the tangle of thoughts and regrets in his head. After a while, he spoke. "You've given me a lot to think about."

She nodded. "It's going to take you time to process. And when you have, I hope so much you will decide to try and repair things with Frankie. Because I know you care about her, and that's the best reason for fighting for her and winning her back. If there's one thing that you are, Nik, it's a fighter; you wouldn't have got through all that you have if you weren't. And if there's one thing she's good at, it's forgiveness. But you have to let her know how you really feel. Be open and honest with her."

"It's a lot to think about," he repeated. He felt uncharacteristic doubt snapping at him. "I am not sure of how I would get her to talk to me after what has passed between us."

"Hmm. You do have a bit of a mountain to climb. Though I think it's more of a case that she thinks you don't want to speak with her. Did you ever remove her name from the villa's title deed or start the cancellation of your agreement with her?"

"No, of course not."

He saw a flicker of what looked like amusement cross Alison's face. "So maybe there's your route back, or at least a way to start a conversation. She's arriving home on Sunday. You could tell her you've had a chance to think some more, and the property partnership is still on if she's willing. See what she says." She grinned. "You may have to grovel though."

"Grovel?"

"Throw yourself on your knees and crawl."

He threw her a sceptical glance.

"Well, not literally. But you need to be humble. I know this will probably be a first, but an apology would work wonders." Her smile widened as she pointed to the two halves of the spiced bun on the plate in front of him. "Now tell me what you think of my baking."

NIK PULLED UP the Spider in front of the gates to his house and aimed the remote at them. They opened, and he guided the car onto the front driveway. He picked up the food container from the passenger seat containing the spiced buns that Alison had pressed on him before he'd left her house. The bun he'd sampled had been delicious, and he was happy to take the remainder with him so he could share them out with the men who'd be on his shift tomorrow at the *klimakia*.

After letting himself into the house and heading for the kitchen, he poured himself a Metaxa and then went out to sit on the patio to catch the last of the afternoon sun and think. He felt an increasing heaviness weigh down on him. The nights were drawing in now, and the holiday season would be over in three weeks. He'd seen thirty-five summers; most of them had been good, but a couple had been the worst times of his life: when Drusilla had passed away, her heart well and truly broken after Marco's disappearance, and when Natassia had ditched him for Christos weeks before their wedding. Alison's frank advice of this afternoon came back to him. *You haven't healed. Let it out, share it, make your own particular peace with it.* Suddenly, without warning, his eyes filled with moisture and his throat closed up. He tried to battle the overwhelming sadness that swept through him, but the force of it was too much and he gave way to weeping quietly.

After a while, a sense of calmness descended, if mixed with a little sorrow. He thought of the girls to whom he'd offered good times, seductive words, and sex over the last ten summers, but never really given anything of himself. He'd told himself that none of them had wanted more, even though he'd sometimes caught glimpses of rejection in their expressions when he'd sent them on their way the morning after the night before, or at the end of their vacations. He downed the remainder of his Metaxa and wiped his mouth with the back of his hand. Things were different now. This summer had been the best of his life so far because of Frankie. Even those early weeks when they'd clashed every time they'd met had been exhilarating. She'd been honest and real in her emotions and reactions and he'd responded in kind, because he'd wanted her so much, forgetting his usual reserve and control. She'd offered him a freedom he hadn't enjoyed in years.

His spirits lifted again, and renewed determination powered up inside him. Alison was correct; he was letting this wonderful woman slip through his fingers. He would get Frankie's forgiveness, make her his again… He just had to find a way to get her to hear him out.

Chapter Seventeen

FRANKIE STOOD ON the main deck of the ferry, watching the port of Piraeus recede into the distance. She hadn't been able to get a direct flight to Kathos, so she'd caught a plane to Athens, and now she was on the final leg of her journey home by boat. *Home.* The island was her home now, even though she wasn't returning to what she'd expected. She'd be starting from scratch. She sighed to herself. There was no way she could afford to contest Nik over cancelling their contract. The thought that she'd not get to briefly own and work on the Villa Lemoni left a lump in her throat. But it was no good crying over spilt milk. She preferred to count her blessings; she was well on her way now to getting divorced and being a free agent, and she would be receiving funds in the not-too-distant future; her property dream wasn't extinguished, just postponed. She was grateful she had somewhere nice to live, thanks to Ali and Pav. So she had enough to begin again, even if it might be a little harder than she had anticipated. Perhaps, for the time being, she could find a job working for a local real estate agency or property development company. She would just have to learn more

Greek.

The journey across the Ionian Sea gave her time to relax on the ferry's sunny upper deck and let the stresses of having spent the last week winding up her life in England melt away. It had been good to see her parents, and sad to say goodbye to them and remaining friends and colleagues, though promises had been made that all would come out to Kathos to visit. She thought of Hannah Oliver, the bright, bubbly, platinum blonde who had been her and Andrew's assistant at the estate agency. Hannah had stayed on at McKnight's, but was clearly finding it hard going now that Miss Becky was in the ascendant. Andrew's fiancée had morphed into a bossy little madam, treating Hannah like her personal slave, and there were still weeks to go before Becky went on maternity leave. Hannah had been visibly subdued, and Frankie was upset for her. If only Nik hadn't ended their relationship, she might have suggested Hannah take a break and come out to Kathos. Asked Nik if he could give Hannah a job in one of his establishments. Maybe, in time, she could give Hannah a position in her own property company.

Nik. Her heart fluttered like it did every time he sprang to mind. In quieter moments, she'd forgotten her anger and ached for him like crazy while she'd been away, longing to be back in his arms, and cried herself to sleep. How had it all gone so badly wrong? Why had he misinterpreted her motives with regard to Andrew so badly? Why had she been so stupid as to bring up Natassia when she didn't know the full story? Her eyes filled with tears. She brushed them away. So many questions for which she had no good answers. She'd lost him, just when she'd started feeling so very deeply for him. She let out a ragged breath. So much for her silly fantasies about building a new life with Nik. No, she had lost him, and that was something she'd just have to live with. He'd been so adamant they were through, and his lack of faith in her meant she couldn't go back. She had to put him behind her. Somehow. It was going to be hard in a small place like Agia Kalamaros.

Three hours later, the ferry docked at Paragolis. She queued with the other foot passengers to leave the boat, her wheelie suitcase by her side. Pavlos was coming to pick her up, so once she'd disembarked, she looked around for the Land Rover. There was no sign. Perhaps he'd been held up on the way over the mountain. She decided to scan the harbour side once more before phoning Alison to check if there was a problem. Still no Pav, but on the far side, her heart missed a couple of beats when she caught sight of a familiar figure standing out from the crowd, tall and dark, wearing his customary sunglasses and leaning against his four-wheel drive. Who was Nik meeting off the ferry?

Panic gripping her, she desperately looked for a way to sidle off to the other side of the dock before he saw her. Hopefully, he would ignore her, but if he didn't, well, she just couldn't face dealing with him right now.

"Frankie! Where are you going?" He strode towards her.

She halted and feigned surprise. "Oh! Hi, Nik," she said as brightly as she could manage. "I was looking for Pavlos. Have you seen him at all? He was supposed to be picking me up." She could feel herself tensing up and her skin get hot and clammy beneath her light cotton dress. He was looking as gorgeous as ever, dressed in a shirt and jeans, with a day's scruff of beard. Her insides reacted instinctively and instantly, adding to her discomfort.

He removed his sunglasses and scrutinised her, which only increased her heart rate. "Pavlos is not coming, *pethi mou*. I will be driving you home."

Her breath caught in her throat. What was going on? A stream of questions came pouring out. "You're driving me...? What happened to Pav? Why isn't he here? Why didn't somebody call or text me to let me know?"

Nik didn't reply immediately, but instead leaned in to take the handle of her suitcase, his fingers brushing against her hand and lingering for a second, sending a tingle up her arm. He straightened up. "I arranged with Alison and Pavlos that I would collect you. I wish to talk to you." He let go of the suitcase for seconds to put his sunglasses back on and turned. "Are you coming?"

Feeling confused and wary, her legs weak and trembly as the shock of seeing him again set in, she stumbled after him and her luggage to his vehicle. When they'd both got in and fastened their seatbelts, she found her voice. "What do you want to talk about? I thought it was all over, that you had nothing more to say to me?"

He fired the engine. "We will stop off at a taverna I know on the mountain for an early dinner," he said in a matter-of-fact tone.

She bridled. He was back to his old arrogant self! "You haven't answered my question, and I'm very tired. I left my parents' house at five AM this morning for a four-hour flight, and I've just made a three-hour ferry crossing. I need to go home, have a shower, and get to bed. Can't you just drive me back to Agia Kalamaros and say what you have to on the way there?" She knew she sounded peevish, but she was genuinely exhausted and getting increasingly frustrated to know what he wanted with her.

He kept his eyes on the road. "I will not keep you out late. I am just asking you to have dinner with me so that we can talk for a while."

She leaned an elbow against the car window and frustratedly rubbed her hand across her forehead. Clearly, she didn't have much choice. "Whatever. But don't blame me if I fall asleep face down in my meal."

He glanced at her. "I am sure I will be able to keep you awake, *agapimeni mou.*"

She glared at his profile as he returned his attention to the road in front of him. What did that mean?

They wound their way up a steep mountain road until they reached the tavern, just outside the village of Skalos. As it was early evening, there were no other diners present yet.

They were shown to a table on a pretty veranda filled with terracotta pots of pink, red, and white pelargoniums. Frankie couldn't help letting her shoulders drop a little and some of her tension ebb away as she took in the spectacular view of the valley below and the sea beyond. She breathed in the fresh mountain air and was quickly absorbed by the soothing sounds of cicadas and crickets basking in the mellow early evening sunshine.

Nik held out her chair for her to sit down. "I think you are glad to be back," he observed, moving to sit down opposite her and pour white wine from the chilled carafe that was waiting for them on the table.

She gratefully sipped some of the cool, fruity vintage and nodded. "I was just thinking on the ferry that I've come home."

He smiled. "So you are here to stay?"

"There's nothing to keep me back in England now, despite what you may think," she responded.

He didn't reply straightaway but steepled his fingers in front of him in that way he had when he was weighing things up. "You have wrapped up everything you need to with Andrew?"

It struck her that this was the first time she'd heard him use Andrew's name. Before this, it had always been *your husband*. "Yes," she confirmed, not wanting to elaborate as she wondered where this line of questioning might be leading.

She had to wait to find out because the waiter came to take their orders. She opted for a Greek salad and rice; she was too tired to eat a big meal. Nik chose lamb *kleftiko*.

He turned his attention back to her. "You did not tell me that Andrew's girlfriend is pregnant."

"No, I guess I didn't." She gave him a curious glance. "Was it Alison who told you?"

"She mentioned it when we were talking during the week."

"Okay. She told me you had dropped by."

"I feel it is regrettable that I did not know."

He sounded stiff and…she felt as if he could be reprimanding her. She sensed her tension rise again. "I found it hard to think about, let alone talk about it. But did it matter that I didn't tell you? It had no real bearing on you or us." *Us*. She felt a huge pang as she remembered that temporary, wonderful state of being.

His expression sobered. "If I had known, I could have supported you. And I would not have jumped to the wrong conclusion about you and Andrew."

She couldn't restrain the hot ball of emotion that caught her unawares and burst up inside her. "Are you saying it was my fault you jumped to that conclusion? Oh, for goodness' sake, Nik! Okay, I didn't tell you about Becky, but so what? The point is, you acted as judge and jury and decided I was guilty!"

He leaned forward, consternation in his expression, his

palms outstretched. "*Pethi mou*, listen to me. I am not blaming you. What I am trying to say to you is that I reached the wrong conclusion. I owe you an apology."

"Too damn right you do," she bit out. Then it hit her that he'd actually said sorry. "But thank you for the apology," she added more quietly, amazed he had done that.

"I misunderstood a lot of things," he said softly. "But I would like to hope that it has not completely ended things between us."

His statement pulled her up short. What was he saying? Her defences, already sensitive, instantly sprang onto red alert. "Nik, now I really don't understand. You were so adamant that you wanted me gone, and that you'd be severing the business ties between us."

"I did not actually go ahead and do that," he admitted. "You own the Villa Lemoni. The sale has gone through. You are named on the title deed, and our agreement is still in place." He smiled ruefully. "I have had time to reflect, and I would like to suggest that we resume our partnership."

"Our partnership?" she echoed, completely taken aback. Was he seriously thinking they could just slip right back into being together again?

"Rebuilding and selling your villa." He focused on her with his liquid chocolate gaze.

She hesitated. *Your villa.* She felt a spark of excitement ignite in her at the prospect that the Lemoni project hadn't been snatched away from her, and they might be able to do what they'd planned with it after all. But could she go back to working with him after what had been said and done? Could she trust him any more? Did he really trust her? And wouldn't it be temptation for both of them, which wouldn't be wise or right? She puffed out her cheeks and expelled a breath. "I don't know, Nik. It's just not that easy. How we parted was brutal and unfair, as far as I was concerned—you didn't listen to me when I tried to tell you the truth and jumped to conclusions. I'm not sure I have confidence in you—us—anymore, and that's no basis for a business partnership. Maybe it's better that we go our separate ways."

NIK'S INSIDES TWISTED. He'd been hoping she'd jump at the opportunity to resume work on the villa at least. And that would have been his starting point to rebuilding their physical relationship. But now as he surveyed her poker face, which had returned after weeks of absence, he realised just how much he'd hurt her. She'd said she wasn't sure if she had confidence in him. That hurt him. He picked up the wine bottle and refilled their glasses. Alison's wise words came back to him—*let her know how you really feel. Be open and honest with her*. He felt uneasy; it had been so long since he'd shared his feelings with a woman.

"Do I take it from your silence that you were expecting me to leap at the chance of starting back on the villa?"

He took the plunge into openness and honesty. "I was hoping that you would say yes." He reached out and took hold of her hands. "This is difficult for me because I realise I did not handle things well. But the truth is that I found it hard to understand why you were being so damn nice to your husband."

He felt her fingers stiffen beneath his. "Nik, I've already explained all of that to you." She took her hands away and tucked them out of sight under the table on her lap. "Apart from anything else, did you not see and hear all the other signs that I was wanting out of my marriage?"

He gazed at her lovely face, filled with emotion, the way flashes of pink coloured up her cheeks, her blue eyes sparked wildly and her lips parted. This was how she'd looked when he'd made love to her and she was about to come. He felt his arousal swell against his trousers. He'd missed that—her—so much. "Signs, *pethi mou*?"

"Yes. The facts that I was willing to relinquish my home and business in England and stay on Kathos. That I wanted to get involved with a property project that will take months to complete. Did that not say something about my intentions? Or that I confided in you that Andrew and I had troubles in the bedroom?"

He smiled ruefully. "I did notice those signs, but they did not seem as compelling to me as other things. You didn't leave Andrew because of the bad sex—"

"No, I went because our whole relationship had deteriorated, and then I discovered he was cheating with Becky. But the sex was pretty bad too."

"You told me you were loving him less each day, but that said to me that you hadn't quite stopped loving him completely."

He watched as she nibbled at her inside lip, something just as lovely and familiar to him as her poker face. "When you've been with someone for a long time and loved them, you don't just switch off your feelings for them overnight, no matter how much they might have betrayed you." Her voice and features took on a new softness. "You know about that, Nik. Which was why you took offence about Natassia. You loved her very much, didn't you?"

The waiter arrived with their food, and Nik waited as it was served. The urge to bury thoughts of Natassia, the bitter feelings they aroused, tightened in his chest. But then he looked at Frankie as she sat quietly and expectantly. Even his common sense told him that if there was any chance of them having a relationship, he would have to talk about Natassia to her. It was an obstacle between them. He just hoped she wouldn't think any less of him than she already did when he told her the truth.

As if on cue, after a few mouthfuls of her meal, Frankie said, "Tell me what happened with Natassia."

"Okay. I first became aware of Natassia when I had just turned fourteen," he began. "Her family had moved to Agia Kalamaros the previous year, and she was thirteen and in my year at the gymnasium—"

"That's my equivalent of secondary school, isn't it?" Frankie jumped in.

"Yes. My cousins in America said we were freshmen at high school."

"Okay, so you were young and in love?"

His mood lifted as surprisingly good memories that he had long forgotten came flooding back in. "I think it was more like in lust, *pethi mou*. Unusually for a Greek girl, she had fair skin and very blue eyes. Her mother hailed from Sfakia in western Crete. In fact, for the first year, I walked around with a permanent erection," he said, his eyes crinkling humorously.

"No change there then," Frankie put in, a mischievous smile on her face, forking up some of her salad.

He found himself laughing at her cheekiness. He shook his head. "No, no, I am a changed man from how I was then. I was a horny little beast in those days. And with a tendency to show off. Like many teenagers, I had a scooter, and I recall I would drive up and down the strip wearing my shades and thinking myself very cool."

"Definitely no change then! You still wear your sunglasses at every opportunity."

"I did until I kissed you and they were crushed and broken."

For a moment, she scowled, and he wondered if he had said too much, but then she gave him a big grin. "I guess I asked for that. Go on. What happened next?"

"I went to the Christmas festival at Trapazakia." He felt the happiness drain out of him, and saw Frankie's features also become solemn too, as the ghost of Marco came to stand beside them. His meal lay untouched. "It was when I was caught up trying to persuade Natassia to date me that Marco disappeared."

Her eyes widened, her consternation evident. "Oh, Nik, she was that girl? I'm so sorry. But you got together anyway?"

"She did not say yes to me for a year or two after that. In that time, I became a little obsessed with her. Partly because I wanted her so badly, but partly because if I hadn't won her, the loss of Marco would have seemed even more terrible and pointless."

Frankie's expression scrunched up with puzzlement. "You've lost me."

He averted his gaze and fiddled with his cutlery for a few seconds, then looked up again. "It has taken me many years to admit this to myself, but I think my logic was that if Natassia was mine, then I had been doing something worthwhile while flirting with her when Marco disappeared. It was a way of dealing with my guilt."

FRANKIE COULD SEE his eyes were shiny and her heart went

out to him. She could feel her resistance to him melting a little. "Have you ever talked about this to anyone before?" she asked gently.

"No," he admitted. "I did not talk to myself about it for many years."

"You shouldn't blame yourself for what happened to Marco—"

"Yes, I should," he interrupted, his tone laced with self-reproach. "My brain lived in my trousers, and I had helped myself to the free wine at the festival."

"No," she insisted quietly. "You were fourteen and you were a little drunk, maybe for the first time. You had the hots for a girl, and, at that age, with all your hormones raging, you didn't have it in you to think about anything else."

"You are very kind, but my actions caused my little brother to be taken, and my mother to die of a broken heart. And for what? A woman who, as it turned out, didn't really love me."

"Oh, Nik, that's very dark. What happened happened. You were a boy, just a boy when you fell for Natassia." He looked so sad and desolate she wanted to give him a hug. "I wonder if Marco or Drusilla would want you to go on punishing yourself like this? I have a feeling both would be very proud of you if they were around to see you now."

His expression lightened a little. "Everything I do is for Drusilla and Marco, and Ian too. Just before he died, he begged me to carry on his mission after he'd gone to find out what had happened to Marco."

"Which you have. You've been doing everything you can to discover where Marco is." She paused. "Have you heard back from the police about the remains on the mountain?"

"The local chief called me yesterday to let me know that they didn't belong to Marco, but to a young shepherd boy of ten years old who went missing on the mountain during a storm in the early 1950s. They found some usable DNA inside the bones and were able to match it to surviving relatives who still live locally."

"Gosh, that's amazing after more than sixty years," she said, awed.

"Apparently, they can get DNA from skeletons that are thousands of years old now."

"How did they check the remains weren't Marco's?" she asked, fascinated.

"The skull and bones were too large to be his; they established that pretty quickly. But they had samples of his DNA that were taken at the time of his disappearance from a little sun hat he liked to wear and his bedclothes."

"Oh." The mention of the sun hat was sobering. "Poor little soul."

"I won't give up until I find out what happened to him, Frankie."

"I know you won't, and don't ask me why, but something tells me that you will." There was a silence, and she watched him as obviously difficult emotions flitted across his face. After a while, she prompted, "So you got together with her? Natassia?"

He nodded. "Yes, when I was seventeen and she was sixteen. We had a wonderful year together before I left to go to university in Athens."

"Did you stay together while you were studying?"

"Yes, or so I thought. Natassia had stayed at home to work in her family's hotel business, and I came back to Kathos when I could. After I graduated, I returned home to Agia Kalamaros, with a degree in economics and big plans for starting a chain of bars and clubs. Within a year, *Artemis AK* was open and the bar in Trapazakia my next enterprise. Natassia appeared keen to marry, so I proposed, though I asked for a long engagement while I grew my business because I knew she would want to start a family once we were wed and I wanted to be able to provide for them." He stopped and poured both of them some more wine.

Noticing he had ground to a halt, Frankie peered at him over the rim of her glass. "So you and she were engaged," she prompted again. "And then she called it off?"

He nodded slowly. "Yes, a week before the wedding."

"That must have been awful for you!"

"It was. Because she ran back into the arms of my old school friend, Christos. It turned out that they'd had a fling while I was away studying in Athens, and then carried on seeing one another without me knowing." He sighed deeply.

"I think... No, I know, she didn't really love me when she said yes to marrying me, but the idea of a life as the wife of a rich man appealed. But, in the end, she went to the man she did love, even though he was a humble waiter in his uncle's restaurant."

"Did they stay in Agia Kalamaros?"

"No. She and Christos moved over to Lekopolos, where I hear they have a taverna of their own and four children."

Frankie didn't make any comment for a minute or so. She saw now why he'd taken the path he had since then when it had come to women; he hadn't felt he could risk that kind of betrayal or rejection again. And she, of all people, understood that completely. She put down her fork and held out her hands to him again. He took them and looked at her questioningly.

"You and I have something big in common. Both of us have been cheated on."

"Yes, I guess we do," he agreed.

"It leaves scars. So now I understand why you chose short-term involvement rather than a proper relationship. I shouldn't have believed the worst when I heard about your reputation."

He shrugged and gave a half-smile. "I have come to regret that lifestyle. It was shallow and selfish, meaningless. In future, I want to try a *proper* relationship. To give as much as I take."

He looked at her intently when he said that. Her insides

turned over because she knew with a bolt of startling clarity that he meant what he said, and that she forgave him, and, deep down, she wanted a proper relationship with him too. A few hours ago, she would have considered those crazy thoughts. But now he had opened up to her, shared his pain, owned his mistakes, she had the closeness with him she hadn't had before, and she realised she felt nothing but love for all that was great about him, and acceptance of all that was flawed.

"If I overreacted about Andrew, it was because I thought I was losing you." He gave her another searching look. "Have I lost you?"

Her fingers slipped out of his as she leaned back in her seat. "What do you mean?"

His mouth quirked. "I mean that I don't want to lose you, and I want you to agree to come back to me."

"You mean…to working on the villa?"

"I mean being with me, *agapimeni mou*, as my business partner and my lover. And not just for as long as it takes to renovate and sell the villa; for as long as it's meant to be."

Chapter Eighteen

THE FORECOURT IN front of KATS was filled with visitors of all ages and many nationalities, all enjoying the shelter's open afternoon. Kostas and two colleagues lifted excited children up onto the stationary fire truck they'd driven down earlier, carefully placing fireman's helmets on their heads, which elicited delighted squeals. Alison and Gladys manned the cake stall—fifty cents for a slice of chocolate, coffee and walnut, lemon drizzle, carrot or cherry fruit cake, and €1 for a ginger spiced bun or an iced cupcake, all proceeds to go to the shelter—served to a snaking line of people. Sally had been an absolute gem and rocked up with two giant Russian tea urns, though the tea brewing inside was English Breakfast and served the traditional British way with milk from jugs. She also had homemade lemonade and an array of favourite British biscuits—digestives, bourbons, ginger nuts, and shortbreads—donated free of charge by the mini-market, something Alison cannily pointed out would be a great advertisement for the shop, and so there was a placard on the trestle table proclaiming it.

Theo and Até stood at the entrance to the shelter, Theo

holding a collection bucket where visitors could throw in coins as extra donations. He'd wanted his pet to wear her special knitted doggie jacket today, and had to be persuaded it would be too warm for her on this sunny, mellow September afternoon.

Frankie, along with Pavlos, was doing guided tours of the feline and canine inmates' quarters. She was just gathering together a party to take through to the cats' area when she spotted a face she recognised at the rear. The tall girl with long, platinum-blonde hair and ice-blue eyes had been draped around Nik's neck that night Frankie had gone to *Artemis AK* to apologise to him. She stood out amongst the families, dressed as she was in a crop top that displayed her flat brown stomach above teeny-tiny Daisy Dukes, and high wedge sandals that made the most of her endless tanned legs. Maybe she was a cat lover, but something about the way the girl looked around her with febrile eyes, as though she was expecting to see something or somebody, that caught Frankie's attention.

The group spent about twenty minutes oohing and aahing over the cats, many of which loved the attention, parading about in their runs, tails up, and pressing their noses against the netting and purring loudly. The girl in the short shorts stood back, her gaze often shifting to the door.

As everyone made their way back out into the reception room, Nik arrived. Frankie instantly felt her stomach somersault in that way she knew so well. She and he had become inseparable since she had agreed to resume their relationship last week; they couldn't get enough of one another. But the wonderful thing was, she knew now that she had all of him; he'd said he loved her, and he wasn't holding a part of him back anymore.

"Hey." He came over and kissed her. "This is great. There are so many people!"

She leaned into him and drank in the musky-cologne smell of him. "Yes, actually, far more have turned up than we anticipated. I fear we may well run out of cake soon." As she spoke, her eye was caught by the Nordic girl who stood nearby, her eyes fixed intently on Nik in a way that made a shiver run the length of Frankie's spine. It dawned on her that the girl was here because she wanted him.

"There had better be some cake left for me," he joked. "That is the only reason I came."

"So not to see me then?" she came back. "Ah, well, you'd better get over to the cake stall before it all goes." She gave him a grin. "Gladys told me that she laced the fruit cake with Metaxa."

She pushed off him and watched him leave, standing back to let the next group of eager visitors in. The girl followed him, but not before giving Frankie a glance that would have frozen hot coals.

When she'd hosted another tour of the cats, and seen the party out, Frankie decided to pop outside to get a cup of tea or some lemonade, and maybe catch a couple of minutes with Nik. As she stepped out into the sunshine, she saw Dimitri at the tea table, talking to Sally who, she could see, was blushing up in response to the attention of this handsome man. She waved at them, then scanned the yard and caught sight of Nik in the far corner. He was deep in conversation with the blonde girl. Her hackles rose automatically when she took in the girl's provocative stance; standing very close to him, she was thrusting out her ample chest and flicking back her hair. Instinct propelled Frankie to stride over to join them. "Hi!"

"Hey." She felt reassured when Nik took her hand and pulled her close to him. "This is Elsa."

"I remember you from earlier in the summer," Frankie said.

"Hi!" Elsa held out her hand, and Frankie shook it. "Yes, I was here in June for a vacation, but I loved it so much that I decided to quit my job and leave Stockholm." She smiled, her eyes flicking to Nik. "I start working at *Artemis TZ* next week."

Frankie turned to him, her eyebrows raised in surprise.

"Marianna, our bar waitress there, is returning to college after the summer vacation. Elsa can take over her shifts," he confirmed.

"Oh, okay." Frankie couldn't think of what else to say as her mind diverted into uncomfortable thoughts. It seemed on the face of it a simple explanation. However, something felt off. Why would Nik give *this* girl a job? Then the thought of Hannah, back in England and struggling on at McKnight's, also popped into her mind. She'd intended to talk to Nik about her former assistant and the possibility of employing *her* if she wanted to come over to Kathos. Maybe he could find something for Hannah too. But, whatever, Elsa working for Nik made her uneasy.

Nik pulled his wallet out of the back pocket of his jeans. "Elsa, here is my card. If you can be at the bar at midday next Monday, show this to Vasilis, the manager. I will talk to him before then."

"Thank you!" Elsa glanced at Nik from under her lashes. "I will be there." She turned. In what sounded like an extra friendly voice, she said, "Goodbye, Frankie, it is nice to see you again." But her eyes flashed a different message, indicating she didn't mean that at all.

"Bye." Frankie watched as the Swede bounced away, her hips swinging and her pert tanned buttocks barely covered by her denim shorts. She turned back to Nik. "Are you sure about that?"

He shrugged. "What is the problem? She needs a job, and I need a replacement waitress fast. She speaks good English and German, and says she has done bar work before. Perhaps I did not treat her very well when she was last here."

"Oh, I get it—guilt! Did you sleep with her?"

His mouth quirked upwards at her candid question. "No, *pethi mou*. She was not for me at any point. And, as I recall, I was busy back then trying to win the attention of another, more beautiful woman." He slid an arm around her waist and planted a kiss on her neck.

She allowed a glimmer of a smile herself at his flattery. "Call it feminine intuition, but I pick up that she still holds a torch for you, Captain Kontarinis."

"Holds a torch?"

"She's secretly infatuated with you. You should be careful."

"Call it male logic, but I think you are seeing things that are not there. Apparently, she has brought her new boyfriend from Stockholm with her." He nuzzled her neck again.

"Are you giving him a job too?"

"It was not discussed. I hope you are not still listening to the gossips?"

His words pricked her conscience; perhaps she was being too negative and unfair. He hadn't given her a reason to doubt him since they'd got back together and he'd spoken sincerely about leaving his old lifestyle behind. She rotated so that she was facing him and looped her arms around his neck. "Okay, so I got it wrong. Just an old voice mail playing in my head. Sorry." She stood on tiptoe and planted her lips on his. He responded, gathering her up in a passionate embrace. For a few seconds, the bustle around them was forgotten. "Mmm." Reluctantly, she broke away. "Unfortunately, much as I'm enjoying this, I've also got a job to do. I must away, get myself a cuppa, then get back to the shelter." She looked over her shoulder. "Look, there's a queue for the next tour out of the door."

Chapter Nineteen

FRANKIE WENT OUT onto the balcony and looked out over the misty garden behind Nik's house. October had arrived and there was an autumnal chill in the air; the leaves of the vine that twisted over the pergola next to the pool had turned shades of deep golden and russet, and the structure was fringed with hanging bunches of ripe white grapes. She stretched and peeked over her shoulder back into the bedroom. Nik was still asleep, and her heart filled with love as she looked at him, sprawled peacefully across the bed, sheets tangling around his powerful body. A month ago, she had thought this would never be possible ever again.

She pulled her robe tighter around her; she was getting cold out here. She'd go downstairs and make them some coffee in a moment. She had a lot to do today. She had to clean out the dogs' runs at the shelter, and then go over to the villa this afternoon to meet the decorators and choose paint colours for the interior. That was going to be interesting since she only had a smattering of Greek. But Nik had business to attend to in Paragolis that would keep him there until the evening, so she would be handling it on her own.

No wonder he was sleeping the sleep of the dead—his empire had been demanding a lot of his time this past week or so, and she hadn't seen that much of him.

She stepped back into the room and shut the French windows. The sound had Nik stirring from his slumber. "*Kalimera, ormorfo*," he said groggily, raising himself up on one arm and rubbing his face with his other hand, blinking in the pale sunlight.

She went over to kiss him. When she bent down, he laced his fingers in her hair and gently eased her on top of him.

"You are so beautiful in the mornings," he murmured, his fingers tracing the line of her cheekbone. He raised himself and his lips fused with hers, his hands moving to push her robe from her shoulders and reveal her naked body. Breaking their passionate kiss, she pulled back from him. Shifting back the sheet that covered him, she straddled him. His attention instantly lasered in on her breasts, and he caressed and teased her nipples into hard points until she leaned forward to allow his mouth to carry on suckling them.

His hands went to her ribcage, and he lifted and pushed her onto her back. Then he rolled over and shimmied down her body until his head was between her legs. He pushed her thighs open wider so that her sex was open to him and began laving her with his tongue, coaxing the heat and wetness of her until she writhed and moaned. "Oh, God, Nik."

Just when she thought she was on the verge of coming,

he drew away from her and moved to lie beside her. "Ride me," he whispered. She moved her languid limbs to straddle him once more, and he held himself while she lowered herself onto his hardness. The moment of penetration made her gasp with pleasure as he filled her and started moving, his hands going to her hips. He helped her match his rhythm and she went with him as it accelerated, her muscles milking and squeezing him, greedy for the length and swollen girth of him inside her, and the beckoning intensity of her orgasm as it began to build. It arrived quickly, and as she splintered joyfully into a million pieces, she heard him cry out and felt the hot rush of his climax pouring into her.

She steadied herself on his heaving chest and caught his hooded gaze as he slowed his breathing. "I love you," she murmured.

FRANKIE GATHERED UP the paint charts to take home with her. She and the decorators had got along great. One had some English, and with a mixture of that, a lot of sign language, and pointing at the charts, she'd picked out the colours she wanted for the walls, which would complement the cypress wood floors that were going to be laid the following week, before the painting began. She looked around her. It was all beginning to come together. The electrics had been fixed and the plastering done, and she would choose the bathroom and shower fittings next, then the kitchen units and appliances. Perhaps she could persuade Nik to join her in that, though he still seemed very caught up in his own affairs and happy for her to do whatever she wanted with the interior.

Her phone beeped. It was him, sending her a text message: *Managed to get away early. At* Artemis TZ. *Come and have drinks with me there.* She smiled and a warmth filled her. She hadn't expected to see him tonight, and it would be good to relax with him for an hour or two. She checked the time: five-thirty PM. She'd better ring Ali first to let her know she'd be late back for supper, or maybe not at all.

She drove along the coastal road, then down the hill into Trapazakia in her newly hired little car, the headlights switched on because evening was drawing in, and with the air circulation blowing out warm air because the temperature was dropping. The island was battening down for the approaching winter; the tourists had gone home, and many of the bars and tavernas closed during the low season, their staff heading to Athens or other places on the mainland to take temporary jobs. Nik chose to keep his establishments open all year round, and they served as hubs for the remaining locals. He was smart, Frankie pondered; he knew how to build a loyal clientele. Perhaps he could talk to Sally, who was getting more and more despondent about the new supermarket that would open its doors in January and who needed some good advice. She would ask him this evening about it.

She parked up and then made her way along the harbour to the bar. The outside chairs and tables of the summer were no more. She briefly glanced out to sea; it was choppy and deep grey in colour, and Lekopolos was just a dark looming shape on the thickly misted horizon. She shivered; yup, winter was just around the corner.

The bar was low-lit and quiet. She looked around for Nik. She froze momentarily when she spotted him deep in conversation with Elsa. The Swede, wearing a long-sleeved T-shirt that clung to her voluptuous upper body, while revealing deep cleavage, looked intense as she spoke. As she leaned in close to hear Nik's reply, her breasts strained against her top and brushed the counter. She put a hand up to flick back her long, white-blonde hair over her shoulder before taking it to her neck to fiddle with the silver chain around it. Then her fingers trailed down towards her cleavage. Something territorial reared up in Frankie, and she tried to push it down. But the way Elsa touched Nik on the arm had the defensive feeling fighting its way back up. He didn't pull away. Frankie steeled herself and strode over to them. "Hi!"

She felt a little more reassured when Nik turned and his face lit up in a warm smile. "*Pethi mou*, you made it! How is the villa?"

"Shortly to be decorated in tasteful shades of cream and pale lemon." She looked to Elsa. "How are you? Enjoying the job?"

"Yes, it is good." Elsa's blue eyes glinted like glaciers, and then they darted back to Nik. "I have a great boss." She rested her fingertips for a few seconds longer on his forearm before removing them. "Would you like a drink, Frankie?"

"Yes, white wine, please. Chardonnay?"

Elsa nodded abruptly and set about retrieving a bottle from a fridge behind the bar, while Nik placed a palm on the small of Frankie's back. "Let us go and sit in the corner. I have some news."

"Oh?" Frankie looked up at him enquiringly as he propelled her along towards a table in a candlelit alcove.

As they settled down onto the comfy seats, Elsa brought over a tray. She placed a large glass of Chardonnay on the tabletop in front of Frankie without making eye contact. Then she turned to Nik as if Frankie wasn't there and served him a Metaxa.

"Thanks, Elsa," Nik said. "You will keep me posted about your situation while I'm away?"

Elsa flicked her hair again. Frankie heard her say, "Yes, of course." The girl lingered for a moment. She swivelled her head slightly to shoot Frankie a sly glance, then returned her attention to Nik. "I hope it all works out for you in Italy. See you soon." With that, she swept off with her empty tray, her rear like a perfect pear encased in skin-tight denim.

Frankie inhaled as her head spun and she leaned forward. "Italy?" she echoed, surveying Nik, her brows drawn together.

He grimaced. "That is why I suggested you come here for a drink, *pethi mou*. I wanted to tell you in person before I leave tomorrow morning. I expect to be away for a few days." He reached for his glass of brandy, raised it, and took a gulp. "The police chief in Paragolis called me this morning. A young man in his early twenties has been found wandering the streets in Rome in a confused state. He claims he was abducted in Greece by Romanies when he was a child."

Frankie was temporarily winded by a blow of shock. "Oh, my goodness, Nik," she managed after long seconds. "Marco…?"

Nik's expression became heavy. "Maybe. This person is around the right age and has a few words of Greek, though mainly he speaks Romanian." He took another swig of Metaxa. "Apparently, he says the gypsies kept him captive for years, but he finally escaped while they were travelling through Italy this last summer."

Frankie rubbed the stem of her wineglass thoughtfully. "That's awful. You hear and read of such things… It's hard to believe a child, a human being, could be treated like that…"

Nik steepled his fingers in front of him. "Child trafficking is happening all over Europe, and it's increasing and getting harder to combat with all the migrants on the move. But, for now, my focus is establishing whether this young guy actually is Marco. I am keeping an open mind, but I want to be there to assist with the enquiries and hasten the results. The police here are sending over Marco's DNA records to see if there is a match."

"I see." Frankie reached across the table to take one of his hands in hers. "Would you like me to go with you?" she offered, wanting to help.

He shook his head. "Sergei is flying into Rome from Athens to join me. As you know, he spent time travelling with the gypsies as a kid and has some Romanian. He could be useful." He looked into her eyes and tangled his fingers with hers. "I just need you here to come back to, whatever the outcome."

She squeezed his fingers. "I'll be here," she replied softly. "I hope you get the outcome you want."

"You will be okay working alone on the Villa Lemoni while I am in Rome?" he asked. "I can ask Dimitri to be available to you to talk with the contractors."

"I'll be fine. We've already arranged for the floor to be laid next week, and I've got the decorators under control." She gave a rueful smile. "I was hoping to have you join me in choosing the kitchen and bathroom fixtures, though. I can wait until you're back."

"I think you should go ahead. It will only delay the completion of the interior works."

"All right," she said a little reluctantly. "I can ask Ali to go with me. She'll enjoy it."

They sat for a while in silence, fingers still entwined.

Frankie could see Nik was lost in his thoughts. Not surprising really. If this young man in Rome was Marco, it would be incredible, but also life-changing. Suddenly, her gaze was pulled over his shoulder towards Elsa. She was standing behind the bar, watching them intently. A visibly smug smile spread across the Swede's face, making Frankie wonder what she was so pleased with herself about. It also reminded her that Nik had told Elsa about going to Italy before her. Hurt instantly began spreading inside her. She pulled her eyes away and back to Nik. She wanted to ask him why he'd told Elsa the news first. But caution warned her to bite her tongue. It wasn't appropriate to make a fuss when he was possibly facing seeing the brother he'd lost twenty years ago, and who could have suffered great trauma; it wasn't about her. But when she felt Elsa's eyes boring into her again, she couldn't stop the question that formed on her lips. "What was the situation with Elsa that you were concerned about?"

Nik looked up. "Oh, it is nothing serious. She has split up with her boyfriend. He has gone back to Stockholm. I am hoping she will not follow him. She is a good bar manager, and he is a weakling."

"Right. Um, I thought you had hired her to be the waitress?"

"I have promoted Vasilis to move to Paragolis and manage *Iris*, after the previous manager there was headhunted by a club in Athens. Elsa has taken over Vasilis's position here."

This piece of information rattled Frankie more than a

little. When had that happened? He had said nothing about it. "That's why you've been so busy lately?" she said, trying not to sound too miffed.

He gave her fingers a squeeze and smiled. "Partly." Even in the dim light, she could see fatigue tugging at his features and her hurt subsided slightly. She was right not to give him a hard time. He had a lot on his plate already, and now there was the possible reappearance of Marco to deal with. Though she was certain Elsa had designs on him, he was just doing what he had to in order to keep his businesses running smoothly.

"*Brat*!"

Nik rose from his chair and watched as Sergei strode across the foyer of the Villa Spalletti Trevelli, an elegant, opulent townhouse hotel in the centre of Rome. "*Adelfós*," he greeted in return. "Shall we go straight to the restaurant?"

Sergei patted his older brother on the shoulder. "Definitely, *brat*. I need food. It has been a long day."

The two men left the hotel. It was a mild evening for the time of year, and the streets were noisy and bustling with people and traffic. As much as Nik loved this historic city, he was glad he would be returning to Kathos the day after tomorrow. "So, we have drawn another blank," he said wearily as they weaved around tourists viewing the Trevi

Fountain. "The DNA wasn't a match, and we spent nearly two weeks waiting to find that out."

"The process has been long and frustrating," Sergei agreed. "But it is good that the guy has been positively identified and is to be reunited with his Greek family. I am also grateful to the *polizia* for agreeing to let me talk to Thanos, or Mihal as the gypsies called him, for a short while this afternoon."

Nik nodded. "I, too, am pleased for Thanos and his family. It is something of a miracle for all of them." He dodged a student with a giant backpack. "What did he have to say?"

"Maybe our trip has not entirely been in vain. As you know, Thanos is aged twenty-four, and he says he was four when he was snatched. That would mean he was taken in the same year as Marco. The thing is, *brat*, he told me that shortly after he was abducted, he remembers seeing another Greek child of about two years old travelling with another party of Romanies. He recalls the little boy crying and saying over and over, 'Arcadius'."

Nik stopped in his tracks, shock rocketing through him. "Arcadius? Marco's teddy bear!"

Sergei stopped beside him. "Exactly. Marco's beloved bear. Thanos has no idea what happened to the child, as the Romani group he was with moved on. We should not get our hopes up, *brat*, but I would say this is the most significant piece of information we have had in twenty years!"

Nik inhaled. "It certainly is." He rubbed a hand across

his jaw and stared intently at his brother. "Do the police here or in Greece have any ideas what they can do with it?"

Sergei shook his head. "You know as well as I do that there are thousands of Romani travelling around southern Europe, and they are a closed community. But…" He paused. "Emilian and his group will be coming to Kathos before the end of the year to escape the snow further north, and I will spend time with them as usual. He has always said he knows nothing, and I believe him. But maybe, just maybe, I can get him to spread the word about the little boy who cried for his bear called Arcadius. And then we must hope and pray that something meaningful will come back…"

Chapter Twenty

FRANKIE WAS SITTING in the cosily warm kitchen after dinner with Ali and the cats when her phone pinged. She picked it up. "It's a text from Nik." She tapped the screen. "He says the young man in Rome isn't Marco, and he's coming home the day after tomorrow." She frowned and scratched the ginger-and-white head of Persephone, who was sat purring on her lap. The feline extended a paw and flexed her claws with pleasure. "Poor Nik. Another dead end. He'll be devastated."

Ali looked up from her tablet. "Poor Nik indeed. And Sergei and Dimitri. How many more wild goose chases must they go on?"

"As many as they're called to follow, I suppose. They've got to check out every lead, just in case." Frankie tickled Persephone under the chin, causing the animal to happily knead her claws into her knees, making her wince. "Ouch, cat! Nik's convinced Marco's out there somewhere."

"But somewhere could be anywhere." Ali shook her head. "It's the proverbial needle in the haystack." She gave Frankie a penetrating look. "You've been very quiet recently.

Nik seems like he's been a little elusive, as well. Is everything all right between you two?"

Frankie avoided Ali's beady gaze. "I haven't heard from him much while he's been in Rome, just a few text messages. But I guess he's had a lot to do and think about." She gave a little shrug in an effort to pretend she was okay with it.

"What's bothering you, hun? You were on top of the world a couple of weeks ago, but then I saw a change in you just before he left. Miss Porcupine is back in situ. What is it?"

Frankie marvelled at Alison's ability to read her, and also the older woman's persistence in winkling out the truth. It was no good pretending. Actually, she felt like she needed to talk about what was eating at her, get it off her chest. She took in a deep breath. "I dunno. It's kind of hard to explain. Do you remember seeing a tall, blonde girl at the open day? She was wearing denim shorts—"

"Oh, I remember the shorts. If you can call them that. More like a denim thong. And I seem to also recall a lot of cleavage bursting out of a teeny-tiny cropped vest."

Frankie grinned. As usual, Ali wasn't mincing her words. She could always rely on her to cheer things up with her acerbic but hilarious observations. "That's the one. She's a Swedish girl called Elsa. She was here earlier on in the summer, when she cast her cap at Nik. In fact, when I first met him, I thought she was one of his holiday romances."

Ali raised her eyebrows. "And was she?"

"He swears not. Anyway, she disappeared back to Stockholm, but turned up again last month, and Nik... Well, he offered her a job as a waitress in his bar in Trapazakia. And then promoted her to manager."

"Okay. And the problem is?"

Frankie pulled a face. "I'm sure she's got the hots for him, Ali."

"Ah. You think Elsa has come back here to deliberately target him? And she's already managed to worm her way into his life?"

"Yes, in a nutshell."

Ali pursed her lips thoughtfully. "She was hanging around him at the open day, now I come to think about it. But, love, from what I can see, he's only got eyes for you, and I can't imagine he'd have hired Elsa if he didn't think she wasn't up to the job."

"He did say that he'd had to send Vasillis, the previous manager of the Trapazakia bar, to take over at *Iris* in Paragolis, and Elsa had filled the gap..."

"But? I can hear a but."

Frankie waited as Persephone stirred, rose up, and leapt from her lap, relieved she was no longer suffering the treatment of the happy claws. "He didn't tell me any of this, and I had to find out from Elsa that he was off to Italy. It feels...it feels like I'm suddenly on the outside, and she's—"

"On the inside," Ali finished. "Don't take this the wrong way, but are you overthinking it? The Andrew-Becky affair definitely dented your confidence, but you mustn't start imagining that every man you meet, every relationship you have, is going to end up with you being betrayed."

"Perhaps," Frankie said dully, Ali's words resonating and prickling. "But there's also Nik's previous reputation. It's been bothering me again. Do leopards really change their spots?"

"And do porcupines have spikes? My, you're feeling insecure, aren't you? What's brought this on?"

Frankie groaned at Ali's frank assessment. "You're right. I am feeling insecure. It's just that Nik has been withdrawn again lately, and he hasn't done anything to push Elsa's attentions away. It's almost like he hasn't noticed what she's up to."

"So, aren't those your answers right there? He's been withdrawn, but we know why—staff turnover issues and then the trip to Rome, both of which are pretty all-consuming. I wouldn't mind betting that he probably has noticed what Elsa's up to, and that's why she's still around. He's a shrewd businessman, love, and Elsa with her, ahem, assets, could be a big draw for male customers. That bar in Trapazakia has always been quieter than his other two venues."

Frankie's eyes opened wide as relief washed over her. "Oh, Ali, do you really think that's what's happening?"

"I wouldn't be surprised. Do you know what else I think? You and he need to spend some time together, relax with each other and keep connected. You've been busy, too, with the villa."

Frankie grinned again. "As usual, *Kyria* Angelis, I think you're right. I, of all people, should know the signs—it's what happened with Andrew. We were both too busy for one another, and we drifted apart."

Ali rose from her seat. Frankie watched as the three cats leapt up too and began milling about, knowing they hoped their mistress's movement signalled suppertime. Ali came around the table and gave her shoulder an affectionate squeeze. "Don't be too hard on yourself." She chuckled. "A little bird—well, Sally, actually—told me that Aspasia, Nik's housekeeper, is away this week in Thessaloniki visiting her brother—"

"I didn't know that either," Frankie interrupted, fresh anxiety blossoming.

"Oh, give over! It's just one more thing that slipped his mind because he was taken up with the Rome investigation. Anyway, as I was saying, Aspasia is away until the beginning of next week. Do you know what time Nik gets in on his return?"

"Um..." Frankie picked up her phone and checked his message. "He's flying from Rome to Athens, and then Athens to Paragolis, landing early evening."

"That's a lot of detail from a man who you think doesn't care! So, you've got no Aspasia, and you will have a hungry, tired man who's been through an ordeal and travelling most of the day. Any ideas?"

Frankie put her head on one side, her lips curving upwards. "Ooh, I feel a hearty casserole, a nice bottle of wine, and perhaps some candles and flowers might be in order. He's given me the security code for his house..."

Chapter Twenty-One

SALLY HANDED FRANKIE the last of the carrier bags of supplies that Frankie had bought from the mini-market, and she stowed it in the boot of her little silver hatchback, then closed the rear door.

"The best of luck with your *dinner-a-deux,"* Sally said, stepping back and smiling broadly. "Let me know how it goes."

"I will! Thanks for all your help. You've been a star." Frankie eased herself into the driver's seat, started the ignition, and then pulled away, waving a hand out of the window. She drove down the hill to Nik's house, feeling pleased and excited. She had plenty of time to get the casserole prepared and let it cook slowly, plus perform the few finishing touches she had in mind in time for Nik's arrival this evening. She hadn't told him, as she was looking forward to surprising him. Her excitement rose as she glanced at the small, fancy box on the passenger seat next to her, which contained a set of sexy lingerie, purchased yesterday in Paragolis. She'd also brought along her best black leather stilettos. The question was—should she open the door to him wearing her saucy finery, or change into it later after they'd had dinner? Perhaps the latter, because he would be tired and needing a shower, and wanting food and a glass of red wine…

She pulled up in front of the gates of Nik's house and aimed the remote he'd given her, then proceeded onto the driveway. She got out of the car and went around it to open the boot, humming to herself. Grabbing the bunch of flowers she'd bought in the village and also the carriers of food and wine, she made her way to the front door and let herself in. The security system didn't beep when she entered, so she put her shopping down and went to look at the key pad; it was switched off. *Strange*. Then she noticed a woman's handbag and a rucksack left to the side of the hall. Aspasia's? Had she come back early?

"Hello! *Chairéte*!" When she got no reply, she headed for the kitchen. The unexpected sight of dirty dishes, cutlery, and mugs strewn over the counters greeted her. Eyebrows knitting together in puzzlement and her heart starting to thump, she tried to make sense of the scene. This was definitely not down to Aspasia, who was the cleanest, tidiest woman. *Someone else was here*! She stood for a moment, attempting to rein in her wildly racing thoughts. *Who on earth…*? Then she took a calming breath and got herself under control. This wasn't right. What should she do? Call Nik? She glanced at her watch. He was probably in the air right now, but it was worth a try. Or she could call Dimitri and see if he knew anything. Panic rising again, she decided to go back outside; it was safer out there and her phone was in the car.

She went back into the hall and came to another abrupt halt as she saw a tall, blonde, and very naked woman standing on the stairs. *Elsa*!

"Wha-what are you doing?" she demanded.

Elsa drew herself up straighter and raised her chin, and Frankie couldn't help but notice how the movement accentuated the girl's large, firm breasts. She pulled her eyes away and swallowed, but stayed rooted to the spot.

"I am living here," Elsa replied haughtily. "What are *you* doing?"

"Does Nik know you're staying?" Frankie responded sharply, looking at Elsa again, anger bubbling up inside her now.

"Of course. He invited me to stay."

Shock made blood rush to Frankie's head and she was stunned into winded silence.

"He hasn't told you?" Elsa's eyes narrowed and glittered like a snake's, and she smiled. "I am sorry if I surprised you," she said, her tone becoming super-sweet. "I had to move out of the apartment I was in at short notice, because my ex returned to Sweden. But Nik came to my rescue. He immediately suggested that I come and live here, which is perfect. We've become so close since I started working for him." She giggled. "I've made myself at home while he's been away."

"So I can see," Frankie croaked in reply.

"Have you come for anything in particular?"

Frankie glanced at the flowers and the bags of shopping that lay discarded on the floor, and a big lump formed in her throat. "No," she said thickly, then, suddenly feeling weak and defeated, and needing to get away, she started for the front door.

"I'll let Nik know you called by," Elsa called after her.

Frankie slammed the still-open hatchback door shut, then got into the car, started it, and pulled off as fast as she could. She turned out onto the road to make for home, but had to pull over shortly as hot tears blinded her. For countless minutes, she sobbed her heart out until the intense emotional pressure that had built up inside her subsided. Wiping her eyes, she caught sight of the box of lingerie sitting beside her. She reached for it. Setting it on her lap, she undid the ribbon around it and lifted the lid. She pushed aside the delicate tissue paper to reveal a red silk bra with a black lace trim, matching panties, a suspender belt, and fine black silk stockings. She welled up again, feelings of stupidity and shame overwhelming her. She should have listened to what her gut had been trying to tell her all along.

NIK RAKED A frustrated hand over his hair. He didn't know what else to say to convince Frankie. Damn Elsa—damn himself! He'd been so wrapped up in the events in Rome, he'd reacted without thinking things through.

"*Pethi mou,* I am telling you the truth. As I have already explained, Elsa called me at the end of last week. She was distraught because her boyfriend had left her, and she was being thrown out of their apartment because she could not cover the rent. She said she had nowhere to go, so I agreed she could stay at my house until she found alternative accommodation. Aspasia gave her a key before she left for Thessaloniki."

"Nik, really? You expect me to believe that?"

"Yes! Elsa assured me she would just be there for a few nights while I was away and gone before I got back from Italy. She said she knew of a cheap holiday let becoming free that one of the bar's patrons had mentioned. It was as simple as that."

Frankie blew out her cheeks and folded her arms. "Had you not noticed how she'd been coming on to you before you went to Rome?"

"Yes, but she is like that with every man."

"Oh, please!" Frankie's eyes still glared with fury. "Where the hell is she now?"

"On the ferry to Piraeus. As soon as I discovered her yesterday evening, I called Vasillis, who sent over two of the bouncers who work at *Iris.* They escorted her to Paragolis, Vasillis arranged for her to spend the night in a hotel there, and he and his guys put her on the boat this morning. There is a plane ticket waiting for her at Athens International to fly back to Stockholm tonight."

"All very neat and tidy."

"I wanted her gone as soon as I discovered her and what was going on. She will not bother us again." He took a step forward and reached out a hand to gently touch Frankie's cheek. She moved away. "*Moro mou*, do not turn away from me. Do not let this misunderstanding come between us." He took another step and caught hold of her, pulling her stiff body to him and wrapping his arms around her. He planted his lips on her forehead and murmured, "How can I prove to you how much I need you? That you are who I want?"

"I don't know, Nik, I really don't know…"

Chapter Twenty-Two

THE FIRST STORM of the winter was predicted to blow in tonight; Ali had said it could be quite fierce. It was early on a November afternoon, but already the sky had darkened to an ominous grey-green colour. The wind had got up, too, and was howling like a banshee around the Villa Lemoni.

Frankie surveyed the newly fitted kitchen units and appliances. She felt the glow of satisfaction; everything was looking really good. The tilers would be here in a couple of days to do the floors and walls. But more than that, she'd accomplished most of it by herself, almost without Nik's help, roping in Alison or Pav to translate if she needed them. Since the Elsa incident, she'd told Nik she would work on the villa alone until it was ready to be put up for sale. She was still determined to pay him back, and it wouldn't be too long before she could do that—a Decree Nisi had recently been granted, a legal notice that her marriage to Andrew was to be dissolved, and a date just before Christmas had been set for the Decree Absolute that would end it. A court order had also been issued for their financial settlement. She couldn't wait to finally be free of Andrew, and would feel happier, she hoped, once she ended her obligation to Nik as well.

Nik—a heavy weight threatened to lie on her chest whenever he entered her mind. She was thankful she had the Villa Lemoni to absorb her and drag her focus away from those taunting thoughts. Deep down, she still loved him. But after all that had happened, it was too painful to give that knowledge freedom and let him back into her life, beyond dealings about the villa. She accepted he hadn't intended an affair with Elsa, that the girl had tried to manipulate the situation. But all the same, it hurt too much that he'd allowed it to happen. It felt like he hadn't cared enough to put her first and let Elsa know that he wasn't available. And maybe she'd been shown an unwelcome truth; he thought he'd bought her, and though he might still want her the way one wanted a prize possession, he didn't love her the way she needed him to. So, instead, she was existing in a state of numbness, without him.

She turned off the kitchen lights and walked across the hall into the living room, just as it was lit up by a bright flash of lightning. A long, low rumble of thunder followed soon after, and through the patio doors, she saw fat raindrops start to fall. The storm had arrived earlier than forecast. She had better get going and back to Agia Kalamaros. She went to retrieve her phone. As she reached down to pick it up, the screen lit up: Ali was calling.

"Love, the weather's getting worse—" The rest of Ali's

sentence was scrambled. Lightning flashed again like a sputtering fluorescent light, and there was a loud clashing of thunder overhead.

"Ali, can you hear me?"

There was nothing but crackling. Frankie pressed the off button on the phone. She could see the storm cracking and illuminating the dark sky out over the angry sea with neon forks. Another flash and a deafening clap had her moving quickly to retrieve her bag so that she could leave. The road between here and Agia Kalamaros was rough in parts and could quickly become impassable.

The rain was coming down in stair rods, and water poured off the hillsides and down the road in brown muddy torrents as she drove at low speed to the village. When the entrance to KATS came into sight, she gave a sigh of relief. But as she turned onto the forecourt, she was surprised to see the bedraggled figures of a small boy and a brown dog. She realised they were Theo and Até. As she got out of the car, the child ran towards her, crying his eyes out, and the dog barked frantically.

"Theo, what are you doing out in this storm? What's the matter, sweetheart?" she exclaimed, forgetting in her concern that the boy wouldn't be able to understand her.

He flung himself at her and sobbed, while Até stopped her barking and came to sit beside them.

Frankie bent down and put her arms around the child to comfort him. She didn't have enough Greek to discover what was wrong and why he was here. As the rain sheeted down, soaking her and him to the skin, she wondered what to do. Where was Ali? She must be inside the shelter.

She gave Theo a hug, and then stood up and offered him her hand. "*Ela*," she said to Até. The dog got up immediately and followed Frankie, just as she'd commanded.

Inside the shelter, she called out, "Ali! Ali! Are you here?"

Ali came rushing through from the dogs' quarters. She stopped when she saw the sodden threesome. "What's this?" she asked.

"I don't know. I found both of them outside. Theo's very distressed. Maybe he's frightened by the storm."

"Oh, God. I had no idea. I couldn't hear anything back there, what with the dogs barking and the thunder." Ali knelt down and gently asked Theo something in Greek.

Theo clung to Frankie and started crying again. "*Giagia*," he said between gulps. "*Giagia*."

"What's he saying, Ali?" Frankie asked, her eyes wide at the little boy's distress.

"He's repeating 'Grandma'. I think something must have happened to Crysanthe. We need to get help over to Skalos. If my phone is working, that is. You cut out on me when I called you at the villa." She went to pick up her mobile from a side counter. "Damn! Definitely no signal!"

Frankie dived into her bag and fished out her own phone. "I've got nothing too."

"That can happen here during severe weather. I wonder

if the landlines are working." She moved quickly along to where the shelter's main phone sat, picked up the handset, and held it to her ear. "Nope, that's out as well. I doubt if the phone in the house is on either. Right. Pavlos is somewhere out there with Panagiotakis and Ianos trying to stop a stream flooding the olive groves. There's no way of calling the emergency services, unless we go up to the fire or police stations."

Frankie felt Theo's grip tighten on her. "*Giagia*," he wailed.

"Look, why don't you do that, Ali? Go to the firehouse to see if Kostas is there. Take Theo and Até with you. I'll drive up to Skalos. If something has happened to Crysanthe, I can help her or wait with her until help arrives."

Alison's expression was sceptical. "Is that a good idea? The road between here and Skalos is very steep, and it'll be treacherous in this weather—"

"But if Crysanthe is ill or hurt…" Frankie's eyes went to the distressed child at her hip and the mournful-looking dog next to him. "I'm going," she said decisively.

"All right," Ali agreed reluctantly, "I guess it's the only alternative. Hopefully, there is a crew at the fire station and they can follow you up there or inform the police."

"What about Nik?" Frankie suggested slowly. "He might be in Agia Kalamaros today, and he'll know what to do."

Alison's features relaxed a little. "Okay, I'll call in at his place on my way up to the fire station. Hopefully, he'll be there. But let me lock up the animals so they'll be safe, and then get some towels and blankets from the house first. All of you are wet through."

Ten minutes later, Theo was installed on the backseat of the Land Rover, wrapped in a towel and a blanket, while Até sat on a towel next to him. Frankie peered in at the sorry pair. Hopefully, Kostas would be at the firehouse and they would be reunited with him soon. She got into her car and set off, with Alison steering the Land Rover behind her. Alison forked off up towards Nik's, while Frankie started the climb up along the winding route to the mountain and Skalos.

Alison hadn't been joking when she said that the road would be treacherous. It was a mire of mud, and Frankie had to weave around potholes filled with rainwater and landfalls in places, not to mention she could hardly see more than a couple of feet ahead because of the ferocity of the rain and a swirling mist, which made her very nervous because there was a sheer drop to one side of her down into the valley.

Suddenly, there was an almost blinding flash of lightning, a bang like a bomb going off, and then some boulders rolled out in front of her from the mountainside. She slammed her foot on the brake and skidded to a halt. There were a few seconds' silence, broken only by the pounding of the rain on the car, and then another massive thud as a huge rock hit the passenger side. The vehicle immediately tilted to the left, then toppled over, and her head made brutal contact with a hard surface. The car slid a little further, but came to a halt right on the edge of the road where it fell away into the gorge below.

Frankie lay very still. She could feel the seat belt cutting into her neck and her side and something wet running down her face. She put her hand up and wiped at it. There was another flash of lightning, and she could see blood trickling down her fingertips. Notions of trying to reach for her phone flitted by, but she continued to lie frozen and suspended, not daring to move in case any motion sent the car over the precipice. Even if she had been able to get to it, there would be no signal up here. How long would it take for someone to find her? Misery quickly followed. Her eyes filling with tears, she thought of Nik. How she longed for him at this minute, to feel his strong arms around her, to have his deep voice soothing her and telling her everything would be all right. She tried pulling herself together, told herself to stop being so childish. They weren't even together! But that just made her predicament worse, and she started to sob in earnest.

She was utterly alone up here on this deserted mountainside, with the rain beating mercilessly down. Her head throbbed with pain, and she was starting to feel lightheaded and sick, then so very tired. Consciousness began to come and go, along with agony in her heart, because she realised now how stupid she'd been when she'd refused to listen to Nik about Elsa and sent him away…

Chapter Twenty-Three

NIK HAD JUST finished changing into his fireman's gear. The increasing ferocity of the storm had compelled him to call the *klimakia* to see if he was needed on board. But he hadn't been able to get a signal and his landline was dead, so he'd got in the car and struggled up the hill to report for duty.

He heard a commotion and a woman's voice. Was she a local come to ask for help in person in the absence of any means of communication? The radio had been ominously quiet.

He was surprised when he saw Alison, and then his gut clenched as he thought of Frankie. Where was she? He assumed she was working at the Villa Lemoni. Perhaps she was stranded there because the road between Agia Kalamaros and Trapazakia would be a quagmire by now.

Then he caught sight of Kostas, his arms around his son, who was wrapped in a towel, while the dog sat patiently by. "Kostas?" he called. "What has happened?"

"Oh, Nik, I'm so glad you're here. I went to your house, but you weren't there." Alison came rushing over to him.

"We think Chrysanthe is in trouble. Frankie found Theo and Até in the front yard. Somehow, they must have walked down from Skalos—"

"Frankie, she is okay? Where is she?"

Alison's face clouded over. "She went up to Skalos to help Chrysanthe, while I came here to raise the alarm and bring Theo and Até back to Kostas. Nik, I wasn't happy that she did that, but she insisted—"

A cold, clammy hand of fear gripped the back of his neck. "*O, Thee mou*, Alison, the conditions are terrible up there in this kind of weather. Only a properly equipped vehicle or a four-wheel drive would be adequate." He put on his waterproof hi-viz jacket. "Kostas, we must go immediately and check on your mother, and hope Frankie has reached her safely. Alison, can you take Theo and Até home with you for now?"

"Yes, of course." She turned to Theo and asked him in Greek, "Will you and Até come and have tea with me? I baked some of those buns you like yesterday. Then you can help me put the cats and dogs to bed."

At first, Theo looked a little wary, but then he nodded his head. Até got up and wagged her wet tail.

Nik followed the fire truck in his four-wheel drive through the rain and mist as it lumbered up the mountain road. The whole time, his mind was going around in circles. Was Frankie all right, or had his curse struck again and he'd lost another person he loved? *Because he did love her*! The realisation hit him like a light switch being flicked on in a darkened room. If she'd had an accident… He blinked, trying to wrestle with his fear and get a hold on it. She was probably fine, sitting with Chrysanthe in Skalos, enjoying a warming cup of tea after her cold, wet journey up there. *She had to be.*

He saw the driver of the fire engine extend a hand out of the window and wave for him to stop. He pulled up and got out. He peered around the truck and saw the way ahead was blocked by a fall of boulders. He walked towards them and quickly became aware of a small silver car lying on its side in the glare of the truck's headlights, perilously close to the edge of the road and the drop into the gorge below. *Oh, dear God! Frankie's car*! He started to run, pain squeezing his heart and lungs until he could hardly breathe. As he neared the overturned vehicle, he prayed hard that she was still alive, knowing for certain that he would never, ever again let her go…

Chapter Twenty-Four

THE FOLLOWING MORNING, Frankie lay in a small ward in St. Nektarios Hospital. She'd been a little sick and her head ached like hell, now that the anaesthetic she'd received before her wounds were cleaned and stitched had worn off. Ali had gone to find a nurse to get her some painkillers. Apparently, she'd got a concussion and her face was also badly bruised. Still, the head scan she'd been given hadn't shown any bleeding in her brain. She also had a friction burn on her neck where the seat belt had grazed her. All in all, she'd got off lightly.

Perhaps her lucky escape was a sign, a wakeup call to tell her she shouldn't be a porcupine any longer. All through the terrifying experience in the car, it had been Nik who'd been in the forefront of her mind, almost as though he was there with her...only he wasn't. But could she change that? She'd turned him away, and he might not want to come back. But she had to try to get him back, let him know just how much she loved him. If only she could talk to him right now...

She caught sight of a tall figure approaching her bed. Her heart leapt, and she instinctively held out her hand. *He'd come; he was here*!

Nik grasped her fingers, warming her with his firm touch. "How are you feeling, *pethi mou*?" he enquired softly. "You gave me quite a shock when I saw your car lying centimetres from a thousand-foot drop, and when I looked inside, you were lying bleeding and tangled in your seat belt."

"Oh, I was just hanging about." She gave him a sheepish grin, and then winced because moving her face hurt. "How is Crysanthe? I hear she is in this hospital too."

"Yes, after we'd rescued you, Kostas and the men cleared the road and got up to his house, and they found she'd fallen and broken her hip. But she is in good spirits, and they think she will make a fast recovery."

"I'm glad. Are Theo and Kostas okay?"

"Both are good. It seems when Crysanthe fell, Theo panicked. Instead of going up to Skalos for help, he and Até walked for over an hour down the road to Agia Kalamaros to find Kostas at the *klimakia*. The storm blew up and they ended up at KATS, and...well, you know the rest. Kostas was worried about who would look after Theo while his mother is incapacitated. But Alison has stepped in and offered to do it. Theo is pleased because he loves her cakes and looking after the animals at the shelter. Até will accompany Kostas on the fire engine." Nik sat down in the chair next to her bed and surveyed her. "You have a couple of black eyes. But they have done a neat job of stitching you up."

"The doctor explained that I had a flap of skin hanging down from my forehead. I don't remember much after I hit my head. How did you get me out of the car?"

"With difficulty. The central locking system had jammed. But Kostas and his team did a great job of breaking the windscreen and passenger window and setting off the alarm, and then I was able to crawl in and get you out. But I had to go carefully. One false move and I could have sent us both over the edge of the cliff."

She peered at him through her swollen lids. "*You* got me out?"

"Yes, *oraiotatos*. You were semi-conscious and moving. Once I had checked you over, I knew no bones were broken. I was able to free you, and the rest of the team helped me pass you out through the windscreen."

"Thank you," she breathed, awed that he had risked his own safety to save her.

"There was no way we could get an ambulance up there, so I brought you here in my car. By that time you were fully unconscious and bleeding profusely from your head wound—"

"Oh no, did I mess up your posh upholstery?"

He laughed. "What's a little bit of blood between friends?"

She frowned and winced again. "Just friends?"

"Not just friends, but lovers. And in time…" He paused

and drew her hand towards him to kiss her palm. "Husband and wife, I hope."

Her eyes widened. "What?"

"I love you. Will you marry me?"

She leaned her head gingerly back against the pillow and shut her eyes. "My concussion must be worse than I knew. I thought I just heard you ask me to marry you."

"Your hearing is not affected by your accident. I cannot risk losing you again. I *will not* lose you again. I want you to be my wife."

Chapter Twenty-Five

THREE WEEKS LATER, Frankie sat in *Artemis TZ* with Nik. She was almost back to full health. Sergei had accompanied them after viewing the Villa Lemoni, and Dimitri was there to greet them too. Sergei had decided to buy the villa on the spot. "I plan to spend more time in Agia Kalamaros, *brat*," he'd said to Nik as he'd admired the polished wooden floors, approved of the décor and the kitchen fittings. "Though it will mean having to live near you and Dimitri, I am prepared to make that sacrifice. I need a break from Athens to write music." He'd swept an expressive hand around him. "This is the perfect place to do it."

Now he was busy chatting up the new waitress in the corner, a local girl, who was smiling coyly but clearly lapping up his attention.

"Hey, how do we get service around here?" Nik bellowed in their direction and banged his palm on the table.

"Shush!" Frankie grabbed his arm.

Sergei looked up and said something to the waitress, who came over to take their order. When she had departed, he sat down with them.

"So what happened to that woman—what was her name? Olympia? The one you've been dating back in Athens?" Nik asked, raising an eyebrow.

"We split up a fortnight ago, *brat*. The way is clear."

"But I thought she was the one, *adelfós*?"

"Every woman he dates is the one," Dimitri muttered.

"At least I have women to date," Sergei shot back.

"So you have it all happening here now," Frankie said, jumping in to prevent a sibling spat. "A new house and a new girlfriend." She looked at the pretty waitress who was gathering their drinks together at the bar, with the help of the new manager.

Sergei shrugged. "The house, for sure. A girlfriend? We shall see." He smiled. "Meantime, do I have to buy a hat for your wedding?"

Frankie laughed. "You can if you want. My divorce will be through by Christmas, and I'm also going to go to Athens for further treatment on my scars before the end of the year if they continue healing well. Then we plan to tie the knot at the beginning of January."

"We must drink to that," Sergei replied.

Nik gave her a squeeze. "You will be my beautiful Greek Christmas bride." He planted a kiss on her neck.

The waitress arrived with their order. As she put the glasses on the table, including one for Marco, she made cow eyes at Sergei, who smiled back enigmatically.

Dimitri reached for his Metaxa. After taking a gulp, he

leaned across the table and took Frankie's hand. "I need to thank you."

"What for?" she replied, her brows creasing with puzzlement.

"For taking my brother off our hands." He shot a wry glance at Sergei, who tilted his glass in acknowledgement. Then he looked at Nik. "Do you recall, just before Frankie came into your life, we had a conversation at *Artemis AK*. I said there was a woman out there somewhere, one for all of us. You just had to believe. And you told us you were a non-believer." He raised his glass. "Here's to believing."

ON THE SIXTH of January, Frankie and Nik led their wedding party down to Trapazakia's harbour to join the throng of people already gathered to celebrate the feast of St. Nikalaos. Their marriage would be taking place the next day at the Town Hall in Paragolis, followed by a reception at *Iris*.

Swaddled in the beautiful cream wool coat that Nik had bought her when they'd been in Athens in December to consult a dermatologist, Frankie looked around her. Everyone who mattered to her was here: her parents, Ali and Pav, Sergei, Dimitri, Sally, Kostas wheeling a cheery Chrysanthe in a wheelchair, Theo in his best clothes and with his curls plastered down, and Até with a garland of flowers around her neck. Even Hannah had flown out from England for the nuptials; Frankie was hoping to persuade her to give up her job and come to Kathos to live. Though Becky was on maternity leave, having given birth to a daughter a little early, Hannah still needed a fresh start.

Just like I did, Frankie thought to herself. *And it brought me the man of my dreams.* Perhaps Hannah could be just as lucky. She had noticed the covert, admiring glances Sergei had been firing at her former assistant today. Who knew what could happen next?

She gazed up at Nik, dark and handsome by her side. He caught her glance and turned to her, his fingers going up to gently graze her cheek. "Happy?"

She nodded. "If you had told me this time last year that I would be standing here and life would be this good, I wouldn't have believed you. But now the dark times are over, and I am the happiest woman in the world."

He smiled. "We have banished nearly all of our ghosts, have we not, *pethi mou*?"

"Almost. But there is still one we have to lay to rest." She turned to Ali, who was holding a wreath of flowers entwined with blue and white ribbons. The older woman handed it over, and Frankie took a step forward so that she stood at the harbour wall. "Here's to St. Nikolaos and all the souls of the seafarers. But also to St. Phanourios, the patron saint of lost things. Perhaps he will hear our plea and bring Marco back to us."

She flung the wreath out onto the water, and the group

watched in silence as it bobbed and floated next to the other floral tributes.

Nik stepped forward and slid his arm around her. She rested her head on his shoulder. "He's out there somewhere, *pethi mou*, I am sure of it. With you by my side, I will not give up until he is found..."

The End

Look out for The Russian's Pleasure Proposition*—Hannah and Sergei's story—coming soon!*

The Greek Island Millionaires

Book 1: *The Greek's Bedroom Bargain*

Book 2: *The Russian's Pleasure Proposition*

Available now at your favorite online retailer!

More by Joanne Walsh

The Italian's Passion

The Italian's Christmas Bride

The Unexpected Bride

Available now at your favorite online retailer!

About the Author

Joanne Walsh became hooked on romance when her grandma gave her a copy of *Gone with the Wind* for her birthday. The teachers at her strict girls' school didn't approve of a ten-year-old reading such a 'racy' novel and confiscated it. But Joanne still became a voracious romance reader and, later, an editor for one of the world's leading women's fiction publishers, where she could do two of her favorite things: work with her beloved alpha-male heroes and spend time in the USA. These days, Joanne lives in the south of England and divides her time between freelance editing, writing and spending time with her very own real-life alpha…

Thank you for reading

The Greek's Bedroom Bargain

If you enjoyed this book, you can find more from all our great authors at TulePublishing.com, or from your favorite online retailer.

TULE

PUBLISHING

Printed in Great Britain
by Amazon

46655753R00138